PATRICK MANN is the pseudonym of a former US Army Intelligence agent who has for many years been a crime reporter for a nationwide American newspaper syndicate.

He has worldwide contacts with the underworld and with law enforcement authorities.

He is the author of *The Vacancy* and *Dog Day Afternoon* – the award-winning film starring Al Pacino.

Patrick Mann

Steal Big

MAYFLOWER
GRANADA PUBLISHING
London Toronto Sydney New York

Published by Granada Publishing Limited
in Mayflower Books 1979

ISBN 0 583 12897 1

First published by Hart-Davis, MacGibbon Ltd 1978
Copyright © Granada Publishing Limited 1978

Granada Publishing Limited
Frogmore, St Albans, Herts AL2 2NF
and
3 Upper James Street, London W1R 4BP
1221 Avenue of the Americas, New York, NY 10020, USA
117 York Street, Sydney, NSW 2000, Australia
100 Skyway Avenue, Toronto, Ontario, Canada M9W 3A6
110 Northpark Centre, 2193 Johannesburg, South Africa
CML Centre, Queen & Wyndham, Auckland 1, New Zealand

Made and printed in Great Britain by
Richard Clay (The Chaucer Press) Ltd
Bungay, Suffolk
Set in Linotype Baskerville

Granada Publishing ®

CHAPTER ONE

The head waiter at La Place ushered in three men with that smooth combination of camaraderie and toadying that is the hallmark of modern American social life. We all do it. We don't have to be head waiters.

I looked up from my drink in time to see him seat the men at a 'good' table. La Place is a membership club; there are no 'bad' tables, but some just naturally have a better view than others.

The shorter of the three men – slim and dark, wearing an off-white suit the precise colour of heavy cream – didn't want the 'good' table. He chose one nearer the disco room, where the sight-lines weren't as broad but the noise was louder.

I glanced at my companion. She hadn't even seen the three men come in. I don't suppose, even if I'd told her who the slim man was, that she'd have been too interested. I was.

It's bloody amazing the people who pop up in New York social circles. If I'd run into Adolf Hitler at a cocktail party, it wouldn't have been much more surprising than seeing the man in the cream-coloured suit, walking freely about town and welcomed at La Place like a founding member.

I suppose that's what makes New York the permanent revolving bedlam it is. The city takes in everybody, anybody. Even a man like the one who'd just walked into the club.

It's taken me in, too, and that's no small accomplishment. I'm part of the social scene here, whatever that's worth, at least for those months of the year I'm in New York. A city that would let me freely circulate in its arteries has got to be a very careless city, or one so free-form that it transcends its own components.

It began that night in New York when I saw the man in the expensive off-white suit, looking tanned and fit and very smiley-white in the teeth. He had a lot of teeth. And knew how to use them. I suppose it is New York's great good fortune that what happened as a result of my seeing him took place three thousand miles away.

New York was spared. London wasn't. To understand how New York got lucky and London didn't, you have to know a little about me.

CHAPTER TWO

To think of one's life as a disposal problem is hardly pleasant.

This is not unrelated to what civic authorities do with garbage. Atomic energy plants have the same problem with radioactive waste. A disposal problem exists wherever one finds material that cannot be left about as is.

In my case, Intelligence apparatuses often have the grave problem of personnel who have outlived their usefulness, know too much and can't be left about as is.

There comes a time when whatever it was that first propelled an agent into Intelligence work sickens within him and dies. If he's lucky, his superiors don't notice this right away.

I was very lucky. I saw what happened long before my bosses did. It gave me time to find a way of staying alive.

What I've worked out is a temporary standoff between me and those for whom I'm a disposal problem. But life is only a temporary arrangement anyway, so I don't see much to complain of.

And there is no rule, in arranging such a truce, that says one has to live in squalor. Quite the contrary: one should join the best clubs, travel to the most attractive places and know the most interesting people.

The club I was visiting this particular evening was not, however, just a watering hole for interesting people. I'd joined La Place for other reasons.

La Place is in the East Fifties of Manhattan. It's not unlike private clubs anywhere else in that the food is only

7

edible and the service only civil. The music is mind-shatteringly loud, but only in the room where people dance. Elsewhere, however, the music gives one privacy, which is important. In fact, disco music seems to have been designed to make sure the people at the next table can't hear a word one's saying.

Like all these places, La Place carries a cachet of in-ness. People pay a stiff annual fee as an act of self-reward, the prize one presents oneself for having Made It. People interested in Making It are interesting to me.

It's useful to be among the successfully self-deluded. In their upward striving, they attract to them or create around them a certain kind of aura. Let's call it a state of high risk.

This is very American. Our society was founded by takers of high risks. To this day, we advance in sometimes awkward lurches by accepting risks that are often immoral and usually illegal. Not every member of La Place recognizes his or her motives this clearly.

In life, the great thing is recognizing motive. It's almost the only thing, that and luck and quite a bit of sheer bloody nerve. The nerve I had. Uncle had made me prove it time and again. Having that, I risked the rest.

Perhaps it's time for a more formal introduction. In these pages I am known as Max Patrick. At least, most of the time.

If you read suspense novels, you know who Max Patrick is. His writing is Average Readable, I would say. But the expertise is flawless. I will never get a Nobel for Literature. But perhaps some day they will let me have one for Truth. Uncle taught me about truth. I owe Uncle a lot.

If I've had some success, it's been because of his training. And if from time to time I seem to be less than I am, or perhaps someone else, or a third person who is only dimly perceived even by himself, this too can be blamed on Uncle. Convenient whipping boy.

I began with Uncle about the time of the Korean conflict. Everything tracks back to that. I had graduated from

8

college and been drafted into an Air Force training programme that produced second lieutenants who did photo-reconnaissance work.

Spy planes at lofty altitudes tirelessly crossed the skies of the planet every day, snapping pictures. They still do. It was our job to make sense of what the sky cameras saw. I had another name in those long-ago days, not Max Patrick. It doesn't matter what.

What matters is that the work I did was normal, part of an official government effort, secret but not illegal, and terribly patriotic. Out of that blameless combination comes many things, including me.

I was twenty-one years old then and a terrible baby about the world and its works.

My Uncle Sam taught me the rest. When Korea was over, we all moved in different directions. Some went back to civilian life, some remained to fight in Vietnam. Others moved into the CIA. A few, like me, shifted sideways from Air Force Photo Reconnaissance into Air Force Intelligence.

I suppose it's generally understood by now that Uncle has spies almost anywhere federal employees exist. The FBI and CIA webs are known, as are the usual military intelligence networks. But it's only the tip of an iceberg miles deep and totally hidden.

There isn't a bureau, an agency, a cabinet post or facility of the federal government – and I do mean such slightly ludicrous entities as the Department of Agriculture or the Bureau of Bird Migration – that doesn't have its own people who eavesdrop and commit to paper vast reams of confidential nonsense. But along with these spies, working in their shadow, are the agents in the field. A different breed.

I began in field work, dirty tricks, the whole package. It's dangerous and one learns soon enough whether one is any good at it. I was. It's useless to speculate, at this late date, whether the right man comes to such work, or the work creates the right man out of basic raw material.

9

All I know is that I took to field work and soon made a name at it.

It's a game of fake identities, cover names and occupations, designed to get one where the job is. Once the information's secured, or whatever the objective of the mission, the whole carefully faked façade of identity is allowed to crumble and self-destruct.

So one month I'd be a family man, possibly a journalist newly assigned with my wife – another agent – to file stories for some newspaper or wire service back in the States. By the end of the year I would have changed hair colour, grown a moustache and would be a field geologist apparently mapping terrain for an oil company.

To be good at this sort of work it isn't enough that Intelligence provides one with an absolutely genuine fake passport, driver's licence, birth certificate, even college diplomas and letters of recommendation from previous employers. That's window dressing. What counts is the man inside.

Some of us, as I say, got very good at it. We were the ones – I can say this now because I've only recently realized it myself – who had no strong sense of who we had been in civilian life. We'd come into the work new-born, so to speak, and it bothered us not at all to be re-born every year or so.

In recruiting field agents, Intelligence managers try to get them young, before the ego-structure is gummed up with self-knowledge. As one ages into the work and proves good or bad at it, a process of natural selection takes over. The good agents get even better. The bad ones die. In essence, they get themselves killed either through ineptitude or sheer bad luck.

After some years of this sort of thing, my superiors realized that nobody could continue enjoying the run of luck I'd had. To give the law of averages a chance to recycle, they brought me in out of the cold and stuck me behind a desk to write reports.

It was a bad time. The man who'd been everything

under a dozen fake personalities was now me. It was devastating. There *was* no me.

You who have always been you will not be able to follow this too well, which is a pity. You will see me in my Captain's uniform – I'd gone up a bit in the hierarchy – sitting at a desk deep in the Pentagon dictating classified material into a recorder, revising the typed transcriptions, erasing the tapes and neatly packaging for our Top Secret files great chunks of clandestine history. You will see a man who obviously is somebody.

But he was nobody, and it hurt. I was almost thirty at that point, always a dangerous time of self-examination. A man approaching thirty will ask himself what he's accomplished so far that justifies his place on earth. He'll wonder where he went wrong and whether he'll ever amount to anything.

He'll torment himself with this sort of thing and eventually come to some compromise with reality. I had hoped to be This, but I have become That, he will tell himself. It's disappointing, but there it is.

A man I had once worked with in Hong Kong, a Navy Intelligence agent some years older than I, had put it this way: 'Never underestimate the danger of being hollow inside. Nature abhors a vacuum. Some day, when you're least expecting it, she'll suddenly fill you to the top with all the shit you've been carefully avoiding. And it'll kill you.'

It killed him. Mother Nature had without warning filled him with self-disgust or whatever it was. He laid careful plans to defect to the Chicom apparatus. Thus, he became a disposal problem. He had to be run over by a Hertz truck.

No, I wasn't at the wheel. But I'd rented it.

Never underestimate the danger of being hollow inside. Each day, as I sat in my Pentagon cubicle, I would wonder who I really was. It was a strange, hurtful time.

They tell me that if one loses an arm or leg, the memory

of it is there for a long time and stirs pangs of loss. I hadn't lost a leg. I had lost a twenty-one-year-old human being: me. He'd been erased, printed over, not once but a dozen times.

They call that a palimpsest or, in painting, a pentimento. There once was something different underneath, but newer things obscured it. When too many newer things get in the way, the palimpsest is forever lost.

Examining the entrails of this strange man nearing thirty, I began for the first time to feel the pain of being somebody. My own somebody, not Uncle's. It took months and, in the end, I didn't recover the twenty-one-year-old I'd once been. He'd been replaced too often for that.

Instead, I had an unpleasant revelation. I had no further interest in doing more nasty little things for Uncle. They made no sense. It wasn't a political revelation. It was simply the abrupt understanding that what I was doing was not fit work for a grown man.

At the same time I saw that I would be a disposal problem as soon as Uncle realized what had happened to me. Like any dross leftover, I had to be tidied away. But I was radioactive dross. I was capable of giving off hell's own lot of lethal light and heat. So I had to be snuffed.

There were several ways I could save my skin. I could join the bastards. I could niche myself even more permanently into the Old Boy's Network that runs these things. I hadn't gone to the right school for it, but they'd probably make an exception. All I had to do, really, was to turn in a few of my fellow agents to prove that I really merited being kicked upstairs to a permanent desk job.

Does that sound unreasonably cynical? Or have you ever considered how one rises in a security-paranoid organization?

If I balked at the idea of framing an innocent ex-pal, I had a second possibility: blackmailing a superior. I'd have to find his secret, set up undeniable proof of it and arrange for the proof to be beyond his reach but accessible to the press if I were killed.

Still too cynical a tone? Well, let it rest for now. It's too much to ask anyone outside the Intelligence community to warp his mind enough to understand what goes on within.

I devised a third path to staying alive. Notoriety.

This is the standoff I spoke of earlier. In writing these confidential reports for Uncle, I found I had a certain knack for putting things down on paper in an orderly, readable fashion.

When one remembers that the things I was writing had, in real life, been disorderly, chaotic and monstrous, one realizes that in a certain limited sense, I had a gift. What if I tried fictionalizing some of these exploits, making a novel of them? Would a publisher buy it? Would readers like it? And would I thus move myself so far out of the shadows and into the light that Uncle would have to think twice about disposing of me?

While still working at my Pentagon desk, I tried a novel. It was bought by the first publisher who read it, as well he might. The damned thing was a varnished version of reality, a headline event I'd helped Uncle pull off in Ceylon some years before. Only to an insider was it apparent that my expertise went beyond what had been in the newspapers.

'Startling verisimilitude,' one reviewer put it. 'Knows his spy stuff,' said a second. 'Unbelievable nonsense,' said the inevitable smart-ass third. There then ensued a nasty behind-the-scenes brawl between me, the Intelligence community and my publisher, who hadn't asked anybody's permission before rushing the book into print.

Threats. Counterthreats. Midnight visits. IRS audits of my publisher. FBI surveillance of his love life (thank God he was a single man!). A near thing on the Washington–New York Eastern Air Lines shuttle I was riding one night with a hundred other people, all nearly wiped out when our landing gear collapsed on put-down. Hydraulic system sabotage.

Another near miss in the Hyatt Atlanta Hotel lobby

when one of those external elevators with glass walls started a free-fall with me inside. Cable had frayed and snapped. But whoever frayed it neglected to short out the emergency system that brought the car to a screeching halt at the next floor.

What cooled it, finally, was that the book sold well in hardcover and zoomed to a million copies in paperback.

Uncle laid off. It was an almost physical thing. One day I was being tailed, threatened, harassed and the rest of the business. The next day, Uncle had retreated to passive surveillance – taps and bugs. I can live with taps and bugs. So can you. You probably are right now.

In the end, my luck held. I wangled a discharge without prejudice, moved to New York and set myself up in the first identity I'd ever had that wasn't designed down to the pocket lint by Uncle.

I was Max Patrick, who wrote those strangely authentic novels of chicanery in high places. As long as I shifted locales and changed names in my fictional accounts, Uncle let me alone for the moment.

The Max Patrick identity began to take hold after a year or so. It was the longest I'd ever been anybody. I grew used to being him. None of my new friends knew anything about the people I'd once been. However, it would have been naïve of me think that I'd successfully left the old me behind.

The seductive thing about dirty tricks is that they don't seem dirty at the time. Mostly one follows orders, which makes the tricks easier to do. But a lot is done on one's own responsibility because one gets in a spot – as when my fellow worker defected to the Chicoms – where one can't wait for orders.

The more tricks, the easier it gets to do them because, as I say, they don't seem dirty. Necessary, yes. Even patriotic. Never dirty because there is no objective set of standards against which to measure them.

In one of my lives I'd been a racing-car driver. Uncle's

experts introduced me to a process of the human mind called 'velocitization'.

We've all experienced it while driving. One tools along calmly at 50 or 60 miles an hour and it seems quite normal. Then, if one accelerates to 80 or 90, after a few minutes this seems normal, too. There is no 'red-line' when it comes to velocitization. The mind takes it all and finds it quite acceptable.

So with dirty tricks. The first take-out is never easy, but once the man's out of the way the second job is easier, and so on. Only later, in retrospect, the racing driver asks himself, 'My God, did I really hit 180 on that curve?'

As Max Patrick, I had begun to replay the dirty tricks. I found I could no longer cheerfully breeze through them. In fact, I still cannot describe most of them as they really were, fiction or no fiction. As Max Patrick, I had assumed a set of standards I'd never had time for in Uncle's service. By those standards, most of the things I'd once done were enough to make a goat vomit.

Old selves return. They are like the virus in the blood of someone who has once suffered from malaria.

When they came back, they had the power to make me shake and sweat in an endless fever of terror. Had I done those things? When the old selves returned there was neither sleep nor the possibility of work. Tranquillizers helped, but only marginally.

Here I was, Max Patrick, the successful author. I brought out a book a year. I travelled extensively and added faraway backgrounds to the texture of my novels.

From the outside, looking in, an observer who didn't know the old selves would have called me fortunate. But someone who had to live with me during those black periods – a week or two at a time, then relief for a month or more – would have called me the most miserable of men.

I spent about a year this way, doing fairly well for a

month or so at a time, then Valiumed out of my skull for ten terrible days. I noticed after a while that when I was dropping V I became accident-prone. All my shaving cuts happened then. So did fingers caught in doors or windows. So did bad falls on stairs.

You can account for accidents any way you like, but they're usually a combination of not caring and not watching. Tranquillizer overdose was doing that to me.

A man in my peculiar position – who had engineered an uneasy standoff with Uncle that the slightest bit of grit could unbalance – can't afford accidents. More to the point, he can't afford to be inattentive and uncaring. Uncle hadn't tried for my aircraft or elevator in a year or so, but that didn't mean I could stop expecting him to try at all.

So I gave up Valium for something else, a form of therapy that required me to face up to what I was, when I still wasn't sure who I was.

What was I? I suppose the kindest way to put it – sparing Uncle's feelings as well as my own – was that I was an unemployed, um, criminal. The laws are very clear about what I had been. Only Uncle's gift of immunity from the law kept me from paying the consequences. He'd withdrawn the gift now, leaving the man *as he was*.

When I finally admitted all that, the black nights left me. Instant replays of old selves and old deeds retreated. Four years have passed. I am much better now. Much richer, too.

But nowhere near as rich as the man in the cream-coloured suit who walked into La Place that particular night.

He was medium in height and his olive-skinned face bore aloft an almost knife-like nose, not Cyrano's length, but of the same cutting edge. His lower jaw showed an equal sharpness, not unlike that of a shark.

He arrived with two bigger, younger men in tow, his bodyguards. None of them glanced at me. They didn't look like Max Patrick readers. Nor had their paths crossed mine in any previous life I had led.

But, thanks to Uncle, the man in the vanilla ice cream suit was known to me. I'd seen his photograph several times. His name was Jean-Luc Dorani. He was an important man on both sides of the Atlantic, but more so in Europe. And he was important to Uncle.

At the time I had no idea how important he would be to me. How could I know that to me he would be worth several million dollars? In cash?

Caption of photograph from *Corriere della Sera*, 8 November:

Luigi Almirezzo, secretary-general and past commanding officer of the National Confederation of Patriotic Veterans, leaves La Scala after last night's performance of *La Traviata*. With Sig. Almirezzo are his guests for the evening: General Marco della Tevere, military intelligence; Dietrich Ralf, Pan-Eurasian Credit Trust; Jean-Luc Dorani, French businessman.

CHAPTER THREE

The fact that Dorani had come to a place like La Place wasn't in itself suspicious. These intimate after-hours clubs are usually connected, in a way their members seldom realize, with the carelessly farflung tentacles of organized crime.

We like to think that life is lived in compartments labelled 'Legitimate', 'Illegal' and so on. But it doesn't work that way, even when one goes to some pains, as in a members-only club, to make sure one's members are legitimate people and one's management is also on the same side of the law.

But private clubs require liquor licences and, in New York, as in most major American cities, the licensing is controlled, or perhaps a better word would be supervised, by the mob. I don't mean that mobsters sit on the Alcoholic Beverages Control board. I mean that the board members are politically appointed. In the US, politics is more often than not the visible arm of the underworld, the one people are allowed to see and cast votes for.

So for the head of the Union Corse – a secret conspiracy even rougher and more disciplined than the Mafia – to walk into La Place and be served with a mixture of speed and deference was not a shock.

The surprise was that Jean-Luc Dorani had ventured to this side of the Atlantic at all.

Those who have come through US Immigration Control know that one's passport is scrutinized and checked against a Black Book. In this looseleaf binder are hundreds of pages of names.

It's a Who's Who of drug smugglers but it also contains the names of people with any notable police record, or a record of having protested too often to congressmen, or of having participated in anti-war or other anti-governmental activities. Next to hardened heroin dealers can be found the names of nuns, students and other gritty non-Establishment types.

It's inconceivable that the Ds do not contain Dorani's name. He might, therefore, have been carrying a false passport. But even then it's hard to believe that one of the sharp-eyed officials who routinely lingers in the background at Immigrations or at Customs hadn't spotted such a famous face, even as I had, in an instant.

Which meant that the fix was in for Jean-Luc Dorani, probably under his own name. At the 'highest levels', where the CIA and the Mafia deal one-on-one with each other, using each other's people, equipment, money and plans, the word had been: 'Let him in.'

For that sort of fix, the stakes had to be quite high. Routine hoodlums don't get that kind of treatment, not that Dorani was in any way routine.

And where the stakes are high, there go I. It's part of my new therapy.

In point of fact, I left La Place as soon as possible, wanting to get away before Dorani made a mental note of my face. The next part was pure luck. If it held, I had something. If not, I was wasting my time. Either way, I felt the stakes were high enough to justify some time-wasting.

I brought my companion to her own apartment, begged off and got away before she could realize she was being dumped. I managed to get back to East 56th Street only fifteen minutes later and planted myself down the block from La Place, in one of those unlighted side entrances to an apartment building beloved by muggers who lie in wait for careless passers-by.

I am not unskilled in this sort of work but neither were the two men sitting in the grey Ford towards the other

19

end of the block. I didn't spot them for at least fifteen minutes, but I had the feeling, since I'd come into the street from behind them, that they hadn't spotted me.

We were, as it turned out, waiting for the same man.

Jean-Luc Dorani is a deliberate man, brilliant in his own line of work, trusted in the highest quarters. But not in any particular rush on this night. He and his bodyguards didn't leave La Place until one a.m., he with a young woman, his conquest of the evening.

If Dorani and his party had taken to a private limo, I would surely have lost him while the men in the grey Ford would have lucked in. At that hour of a week night, there are few cruising cabs one can hail and, in time-honoured tones, instruct the driver to 'follow that car'.

But it was a fine night. Dorani dismissed his men – actually not, since they followed him at a discreet distance – and walked off with his lady. The grey Ford gave them a lead of one block, then limped along in the rear. I fell in behind the Ford, leaving me quite far from Dorani. Our awkward little parade moved west to Park Avenue, then up five blocks to the Regency.

Once Dorani and his companion disappeared inside the hotel, the two guards closed the discreet gap they had been keeping and themselves entered the Regency. The grey Ford drove off, its work obviously finished for the night. I spent the next two hours – it was after three-thirty by the time I gave up – assuring myself that Jean-Luc hadn't merely popped in the Regency for a nightcap. The men in the Ford apparently thought so, but that wasn't good enough for me.

I got home at four a.m. and slept till nine, then went to work finding out how long Dorani was planning to stay in New York.

Only in suspense novels of the kind written by Max Patrick does one have a buddy in the Regency concierge's office who, for a double-sawbuck, delivers some useful line such as: 'Dorani? Oh, yes. Suite 501. He's leaving for London on BA 41 next Tuesday.'

But Uncle had given me the basic skills and insights. I know something about the Dorani type of thinking. These are terrifying smooth men, the Doranis of our world, with a great façade of charm and an intimidating aura of latent power. They come of humble origins, even as you and I. They are the sons either of criminals or of poor people. In any event, they have a basic peasant mentality when it comes to money.

The best illustration of this happened some years ago in the States. A man, nameless here, who was the *sotto-capo* of a major Eastern city and handled many millions of dollars a year in cash, was driving his Cadillac over the George Washington Bridge from Manhattan to New Jersey. Steering into the 'Exact Change' lane – this was in the days of one-coin fares – he threw what was supposed to be a quarter into the basket.

It wasn't a quarter, it was a slug. All hell broke loose. Red warning lights flared. Sirens moaned. Alarm bells went off in a deafening sequence. The *sotto-capo* got no further than twenty feet before his Cadillac was halted by gun-toting police.

Well, it was only petty larceny. He drew a suspended sentence and a $100 fine which he gladly paid to get free. But the publicity followed him forever. This millionaire, this financial titan of the American underworld, had tried to save 25 cents by using a slug.

You and I are above such things, of course. But if I knew anything about the kind of man Jean-Luc Dorani was – a Corsican, not a Sicilian, but a mobster nevertheless – I knew he had a round-trip excursion fare air ticket. That meant he'd have booked a return flight for a date in the next one to five weeks.

I began calling the international airlines at nine that morning, starting with the most logical line, Air France, then going through the other A's. I was calling for Mr Dorani who wanted to change the date of his return flight to Europe. The reservationist would punch up the name on a computer terminal keyboard and if any reservation was held in the memory bank it would instantly print out on the computer's television screen.

Nobody had a Dorani. Sorry, but thank you for calling Air France. Air India. Alitalia.

British Airways was more helpful. Yes, they had him, scheduled for a nine-thirty p.m. departure from New York to London a week hence.

'Is there an earlier flight that day?' I asked.

'At six-fifteen, but it's a 707. Our nine-thirty flight is a 747 jumbo.'

I pretended that made a difference and said I would call back later. He *was* using the Dorani passport. He *was* bound for London.

The next week was torture, but Uncle had helped me inure myself to such things. There was always the possibility that Dorani would leave earlier, pay the difference and depart prematurely.

I can't tell you how desperate was the desire to 'case' the Regency from time to time, if not to keep tabs on Dorani then to try identifying the people who were keeping tabs on him. That there had been two men on the job that night smelled to a sensitive nose like fuzz of some kind, local or Federal.

I did return to La Place twice, but Jean-Luc Dorani did not. And I knew enough not to ask questions about him at the club. I spent my time, instead, collecting cash.

It isn't easy as one thinks – unless one's in the crime business – to collect a lot of cash. I had no idea how much I'd be needing in London, or wherever else Dorani would end up leading me. I only knew that if he surfaced in the US with full protection, he was into something very big.

One has to be careful collecting cash. We Americans like to think we live in an open society, free of restraints. In fact our lives are very closely monitored if we only knew it. For instance, any transaction drawing out cash bills of the $500 denomination or larger is reported by the bank to the government, complete with serial numbers of the bills.

If I were to assemble a war chest of large bills to be used later in buying local help I would thus be running the risk that my own government – which was still keeping a beady eye on me – could trace the transaction by the serial number of the bills.

No good. I had to have $100 bills, but here I ran into a second difficulty. All transactions over $1000 – cash or cheque – are also reported to the government. It's not that the banks like doing the added work of informing on their customers. It's just that the government requires banks to do so and they haven't the guts to say no. Nor to warn their customers that their accounts are an open book.

So Max Patrick spent much of his time going from account to account, drawing out $500 in $100 bills. Eventually I had my packet and my one-way ticket to London.

It's a capital mistake in the Intelligence business, as in the crime business, to let someone know you're going to be somewhere at a certain time. If Dorani had any enemies – a rhetorical question; he had dozens of them – they could do what I did and develop a departure time for him.

They could then, if such were their plan, hijack him on the way to J.F.K. International airport, or something equally discouraging to Dorani's health and peace of mind.

I wasn't his enemy. At this point I considered myself his closest friend. Trying to think as he did I decided he'd use the earliest flight at six-fifteen. It would catch any would-be interference off base.

Then he'd arrive two hours early at J.F.K. and zip off to London in a smaller 707 before anyone was even thinking of looking for him. And best of all, he'd be leaving on the same date as the original reservation. So he'd pay nothing extra for the change of flight. Score one for the peasant mentality.

Even so, I knew there could be a great many kinks in the plan that I might know nothing about. Luck had to hold.

It did.

CHAPTER FOUR

I could feel the air pressure change somewhere inside my head as the 707, flying high over Shannon, started almost imperceptibly to lose altitude for its long downward glide towards London.

Before the pilot could light the 'Fasten Seat Belts' signs, I picked up my case and went inside the nearest lavatory, bolting the door behind me and automatically turning on the lights in the tiny cubicle. I stared at myself in the mirror, swallowing against the steady altitude change.

After a fitful hour or two of sleep, my face looked pasty under my usual shifty light brown hair. It's a useful hair colour, either way. In my FBI dossier, for example, they describe me as blond, while my National Intelligence Agency file settles for 'medium brown'.

It's the same with my height, while it is just a hair under six feet. I am described in one of my passports as five feet, ten inches. The Max Patrick one calls me a stalwart six feet, one inch. Like my hair colour, it's useful.

'Ladies and Gentlemen,' the steward announced over the intercom system, 'we are beginning our descent to Heathrow International Airport. Please fasten your seat belts and refrain from smoking.'

I washed my face. 'The pilot has turned on the seat belt sign,' continued the steward. 'Kindly extinguish all smoking materials and return your seats and tray tables into an upright position, ready for landing.'

'Kindly extinguish all smoking materials,' I repeated silently in my head. I wondered for a moment, since words are somewhat my business, what had happened to such homely sentences as 'please put out your cigarettes'. After all, the flight attendants didn't let you smoke pipes or cigars. Did anyone have a lighted bomb aboard? Kindly extinguish it.

I swallowed again to relieve the air pressure. Then I zipped open my case and transferred a packet of hundred-dollar bills into the space between my spine and my trouser waistband, shoving the envelope down far enough that the usual cursory weapons frisk wouldn't disclose the presence of anything more than a backbone.

I'd done the same thing before the weapons search at J.F.K. Airport in New York, where it's done electronically. In the normal course of events, Heathrow almost never frisks arriving passengers, but now and then, in response to threats from terrorist groups, Heathrow can overnight become an armed camp of extremely nervous, highly suspicious soldiers and police.

Not that there was anything illegal about taking $5000 in cash out of the United States. As a matter of fact, that is precisely the amount our all-supervising government allows us to remove from the country without making a report of it. Any more requires a special statement.

The point was that I had already openly packaged another stack of hundred-dollar bills, fifty of them, in my toilet kit. They were there to be noted, if seen. The fifty tucked in the seat of my pants were not. To be seen, that is.

The nameless people to whom these hundreds might go were in the habit of demanding bills of the anonymous $100 denomination, and no larger. The people were nameless because, at this point, I had no idea who any of them would be. But I already knew their habits when it came to payoff money.

The 'Return to Seat' sign in the lavatory had been blinking nervously for some moments. I zipped my case closed and returned to my seat. Outside the 707's window, lying neatly in the slanting sunlight of early morning, the wedges and rectangles of Oxfordshire farmland flashed by beneath us.

The sidelighting exaggerated each hedgerow, causing it to cast a thick black shadow. The landscape seemed to have been drawn in crayon by a talented child with an Impressionist eye for dreamy pastel shades of green and yellow but a determined Hard-Edge tendency to mark everything clearly off from everything else by long, wavering, brown-black borders.

The wad of hundred-dollar bills moulded itself to my contour, pressed between the back of my two-inch-wide leather belt and the second coccyxial bone. After a while I could almost forget it was there. Below the plane, and getting nearer every second, the farmland was changing to suburbia, interspersed with industrial parks and crossed not by sharply shadowed hedgerows now but by wide white motorways already crawling with truck and car traffic.

'In a few moments,' the steward reported over the loudspeaker, 'we will be landing at Heathrow Airport. The weather here is partly fair and the ground temperature is 15 Celsius, 60 degrees Farenheit. On behalf of Captain Mumble and our crew, we'd like to thank you very much at this time for flying with us and to wish you a very pleasant stay in London. For those of you making connections to other ...'

I stopped listening. I was making connections, but not to other flights, only to Jean-Luc Dorani, perhaps elsewhere than in London, where the weather was partly fair, the flight attendant had assured me. Or was this simply, um, British for 'partly cloudy'?

I had to see my London editor, too. She had been expecting me for some time now. The UK edition of my newest novel had been doing so well that there was movie interest and my publisher wanted me on hand for the negotiations. If Uncle ever needed to know why I'd made the trip, this was an ironclad cover story.

Jane Tait was my editor's name. She signed letters

E. J. Tait and wouldn't explain the initials, but I had once made it my business to find out. They stood for Emma Jane.

She was a young woman with three names, each of them four letters long, all forgettable. Three names and quite a lot of editorial know-how for someone just past thirty. More than a dozen years, however, had been spent working for newspapers and magazines and, latterly, book publishers. She was a tall, slender woman with hair my shade and the same untrue iris colour to her eyes – a blue-grey-green.

People called her attractive but, in the five years she'd been my editor, I'd never seen her that way. Well groomed and dressed. But attractive? Well ... if one liked that type.

I shifted uncomfortably. The plane dropped more slowly now, making its right-angle turns of approach as the Heathrow control directed it downward. This was not my favourite seat on an aircraft but it was well out of Dorani's line of sight.

He hadn't seen me, I knew. The lucky bastard had slept through the whole flight. A clear conscience is a blessing. In any event, he was not in the habit of staring about him at his fellow passengers. Nor had I made any attempt to go forward to get a better look at him. Such a man has associates to do his looking-about for him.

Dorani now preceded me by only a few paces as we left the plane at Heathrow and began that seemingly endless trek along elevated corridors and moving sidewalks through Immigration Control to the baggage area. Like me, Jean-Luc Dorani had only carry-on luggage, one piece. Like me, he paused a moment near the baggage carousel looking very relaxed and almost dapper. Dorani was waiting for his escort. I had paused for a different reason. I wanted them far ahead of me and out of the airport before I left Heathrow.

The two men were Dorani's height, each fairly short, but the bodyguards were stocky and thick through the shoulders where Dorani was thin. They were not the men I had seen him with at Le Place. I'd never bothered to research Jean-Luc Dorani thoroughly enough to find out how this elegant Corsican thief had inherited such aristocratic genes. Perhaps he'd had a noble French or Italian father who sired him on a Corsican peasant girl.

I watched them move out of the baggage area ahead of me, taking the 'Nothing to Declare' path. I let some other travellers get between us, then followed. In the busy areas beyond the customs barricade, where waiting people milled about and passengers moved from rent-a-car kiosk to bank counter, changing currency, I stopped to let the Dorani party get outside the terminal. No one seemed to be following him except me.

Cabs stood in ranks. I had the idea that now he was in England Jean-Luc Dorani would have a Rolls or Daimler waiting, uniformed chauffeur and all, even if it were only a rented rig. But I saw one of his guardian angels hail an ordinary black London taxi. As the men climbed in, Jean-Luc took the rear seat while the two associates unfolded and sat in jump seats, facing him.

In an American accent, one of the bodyguards called out the name of a small hotel, Blue's, off St James's Street. I watched the cab pull away in an iron yammer of diesel noise.

I waited for a while so that whoever was tailing Jean-Luc could hop a cab and follow. They'd danced him very close in New York, assigning two men to the job, undoubtedly on three eight-hour shifts around the clock. If they hadn't actually sent anyone on the 707, they'd have someone waiting at Heathrow.

But they didn't. I'm not infallible at spotting a tail; no one is. But I was willing to swear Dorani was not being followed. That meant they already knew his plans and itinerary in London.

This was the first false note, loud and clear, I know that now, but, at the time, I wasn't listening.

CHAPTER FIVE

'Nothing to it,' Jane Tait was telling me in an airy, off-hand manner. 'What better cover story then being an internationally successful writer of mystery novels?'

I nodded, looking vague. We were seated in one of the outside tables of her favourite lunching spot in London, a wine-and-cheese place hidden from thoroughfare crowds in the heart of Shepherd Market. Whenever I arrived in town, there was no question where we ate our first lunch.

Tait's offices were in Mayfair, not far from the US Embassy on Grosvenor Square. We'd walk across Audley Street and at Curzon there were several ways, including a tunnel, to reach the walled-off Shepherd Market. The area had once I suppose been exactly that, although there were signs that then – as now – it also served as a neatly enclosed whoring place for ambulatory ladies and their strolling customers.

There was no mistaking Jane Tait for one of the red-light professionals who occasionally brightened the area. Not that she didn't have her own style of brightness. In the strong sunlight of late April her unreliable eye colour had gone startlingly blue, the blue of a clear sky at sunrise.

Since my last visit, some three months before, she had cut her long, schoolgirl-styled brown hair. It had been flat and silky and parted in the middle, which still became her rather long, oval face, but would prove a bit too youthful in years to come.

Now she'd cut her hair short, had it fluffed out at the

sides and softly waved. The coiffure was out of the 1930s, but so was the mauve dress that clung to her slim body, and her patent-leather shoes, high-heeled with straps across the instep, which in the States we occasionally refer to as 'Ruby Keeler Clogs'.

Over the dress, but thrown back because of the sun's warmth, she wore a bright red cape, fairly short, of the kind usually associated with children's book illustrations of Little Red Ridinghood.

'Better cover story for what?' I asked in an idle voice, cutting my fat French sausage on its plate and spearing a bit of it, British-style, with my fork held upside down in my left hand. I proceeded to shove and pat ratatouille into place on the fork as well, then conveyed the whole freight-load to my mouth. When in London ...

'For being some sort of international crook,' Jane Tait said.

I munched silently for a long moment. Then I made a production of swallowing some of the good, cheap Bordeaux she had ordered with our lunch.

'I beg your pardon?'

'Come on,' Jane Tait said. She had an ear for Americanisms, possibly culled from my own novels. 'Max, you can live anywhere you want and you do. You cross the ocean at will and live here, in France, in Italy. I know for a fact you transit through Switzerland, which argues persuasively the existence of at least one secret bank account.'

'The sure sign of an international crook,' I put in, continuing to eat.

'No,' she admitted, 'but let me get on with it, because I've been mulling it over for months and I'm convinced I'm right.'

I nodded and munched, munched and nodded. Nothing this woman said was going to spoil my lunch in the quiet open air of an English spring with the lovely sun beating down. Nothing.

Jane Tait had a high, pleasant voice, as if Queen Elizabeth had learned, from some anonymous Professor

31

Higgins, to modulate her normally reedy squeal.

'We all know,' my editor continued in her bird-like tones, 'that a successful writer has entrée anywhere. One is seen at Les A here in London, the Palm Beach Casino in Cannes, the Hostaria della Orso in Rome, La Place in New York, even —'

'That's not the sign of an international crook,' I corrected her. 'It's the hallmark of an international, um, vulgarian.'

She gestured with one of her long, narrow hands. 'I stand corrected by an expert.'

Instead of gnashing my teeth, I continued chewing my lunch. Any editor has the effortless power, simply by being alive, to send any writer into paroxysms of wrath. Jane Tait had done this often enough with her insistence on changes in verb tense or punctuation. However, I was damned if I would let her drive me off the wall on this fine day with her theories about my secret life. Lives.

'More than that,' she went on sweetly, 'being a successful writer gives one entrée to the rich and powerful. One has only to talk of researching a new book and all sorts of privileged information is showered on one.'

'Being a successful writer,' I said in a heavier-than-normal voice, 'should also give one immunity from idiots, especially those who have never mastered the intricacies of successful book plotting – otherwise they'd write their own bloody book – but insist on pestering writers with half-baked ideas that just ... won't ... wash.'

'Why not?'

I sipped wine. 'I hate to sound crass and American, but isn't a successful writer already a crook? He steals bits of reality. Why would he need to steal anything else? Why would he tempt fate and the IRS?'

'Because one doesn't report illicit gains,' she pounced.

I shrugged and poured us both some more Bordeaux. 'Spoken like a true innocent.' I did about thirty seconds of holding the glass to the light to admire the colour of the wine. 'The overriding problem of illicit gains is the fear of being found out. Not because the government employs brainy sleuths. Sherlock Holmes has been dead for eons now. But tell me? What percentage of solved crimes owe their solution to an informer?'

She frowned into her wine. 'I defer to the expert again.'

'Nine out of ten,' I told her. 'The cops don't chase clues with magnifying glasses. They squeeze petty thieves till they turn stoolie.'

'Perhaps, also,' she said in a faraway voice, lifting her bright stare to my face and transfixing my glance, 'you kill off anyone who might inform on you. That would be clever.' She smiled at me.

'In which case,' I returned, 'your life ain't woit' a plugged nickel, lady.'

She was silent for a long moment, testing the kidding way this had been said. Then she decided to smile even more widely. She had a lovely smile, especially when she seemed to mean it.

'Some day,' she said then in her nicest tone of voice, 'I shall take great pleasure in getting inside Max Patrick to find out what kind of sociopath is actually hiding there.'

'How d'you propose to do it? Scalpel?'

She shook her head slowly from side to side and the motion, together with a faint April breeze, ruffled her hairdo and made it freer, less calculated. 'My own weapon,' she said then.

The waiter came over to clear our plates. 'We have a good brie today,' he suggested. 'Nice and runny.'

'Fine. You?' I asked Jane Tait.

'Yes, please.' She watched the waiter leave. 'Max,' she said then, pausing for so long she seemed to have lost her thought.

'Yes?' I asked finally.

'Max,' she began again, her glance still focused where the waiter's departing back had been a moment before, 'do you trust me even a little bit?'

I reached across and patted her long, thin fingers, a pickpocket's fingers, but I refrained from saying so. 'Of all my editors,' I told her, 'you are by far the brightest and prettiest.'

'Shit to that,' she said sweetly. 'I happen to know your New York editor's a big, hulking gent. And I didn't ask the question you answered.' Her glance swung around to me like twin laser beams. 'Do you trust me?'

'Of course.'

'I am not talking about technical things, commas, adjectives.'

'Of course I trust you.'

She seemed to grit her teeth. That was the only way I could account for the clenched quality of her words as she spoke them. 'I want to tell you something I've told no one else. Nor will I ... ever. But before I do, I want to know that you believe me and trust me.'

I was nodding even before she finished talking. I suppose, in a way, I did trust her. My criteria for trustworthiness are few. Never being lied to is Number One. Never being deceived or doublecrossed is only another way of stating Criterion Number One. Perhaps there are no other criteria. Jane Tait had never lied to me.

'I trust you on important matters,' I assured her. 'Now tell me what you have to tell me.'

She started to speak, but stopped when the waiter arrived with our cheese. 'Another half litre?' I asked my editor. She nodded and the waiter left.

'Max,' she said then in a small voice, lower in tone and in intensity than her normal tone. 'That novel of yours we brought out two years ago called *There Are No Rules?*'

'Sold about five thousand in hardcover here? About half a million in UK paperback so far?'

'I'm not talking sales figures, damn you.' She was silent again as the waiter brought more wine and went away. She watched me fill our glasses again. 'Do you recall the plot?' she asked then.

I squinted against the strong spring sunlight. 'Something about Greek antiquities dug up in Yugoslavia? Some black market in selling them to otherwise law-abiding museums?'

'That was the theme,' she snapped, turning school-teacherish for an instant. 'The plot had to do with a two-man submarine from Monte Carlo used for deep-sea research. The timetable had to do with giving the underwater team food poisoning so the thief could borrow the sub for one night without it being missed. Except that the thief was careless and left behind in the sub a little chip of a Greek glass krater which one of the underwater people finally identified. And took to the Dubrovnik police. Who turned it over to Inspector Bulic. Who solved the case and collared the thief.'

'Very good. Justice triumphs.'

'You agree that's a fair summary of the plot?'

'As fair as any summary,' I admitted. 'Any time you synopsize a plot it all sounds like hogwash.'

'That's because it doesn't have the colour, the suspense, the menace, the strong characters and backgrounds for which Max Patrick is so well known.'

It was my turn to smile beamingly at her.

She lifted her glass and did a creditable imitation of my colour-testing number. 'Max, dear,' she said then, 'what would you say if I told you that this summer, in Monte Carlo, I ran into a man who works for the Marine Institute there?'

'I would say, um, "fortunate Monegasque", or words to that effect.'

'We did get to know each other rather well in the course of a week,' she admitted. 'Well enough for him to tell me the most amazing story. It took place about four years ago, Max, off the Dubrovnik coast. He was part of a crew operating a two-man sub. They all came down with dysentery one afternoon and none of them went anywhere near their sub till the next day.'

'Fascinating.'

'I questioned him closely.'

'Show him a copy of the book?' I wondered.

She looked shocked. 'I told you, Max, I've said nothing to anyone.'

I nodded. 'It's possible the incident made the local press. It may have stuck in the back of my memory.'

'The local press?' She drained half her glass of wine in one swallow. 'Max, I know you're a passable linguist, but Serbo-Croatian?'

'It may have been in the English press.'

'It wasn't. I asked him. I went further. I checked back issues of English newspapers.'

'I see.'

'Do you trust me?' she asked then.

'I said I did. I do.'

'Then will you please level with me, Max? Explain the coincidence?'

'I can't. A coincidence is a coincidence.'

Her rather pleasant face went grim. 'Let me ask you something else, then. How well do you recall the plot of a novel of yours called *Dead Wrong*? It was the first Max Patrick book I worked on, five years ago.'

I sat without speaking. I knew the plot of *Dead Wrong* even better than she did. It involved a particularly nasty formula for a mood-altering drug. Sprayed over a city or dropped in a water supply reservoir it had the ungodly effect of —. It had been developed by US Army scientists and then stolen by one of them, who'd had second thoughts about such horrors. Then he had third thoughts about making a pile by selling the formula. Torn between idealism and greed, he was easy game for a thief who stole back the formula and peddled it to the US Army. It was a new form of kidnapping, in which a secret was ransomed.

'You do recall it,' Jane Tait said then. She occasionally had the ability to read me, but, fortunately, only to a certain superficial depth.

'I —'

It was as far as I got. Past our table sauntered a particularly attractive woman. Although it was warm, she wore a dark sable coat, cut short to show a heart-stopping pair of legs from well above the knee. Her black hair was only a shade darker than the sable and, even behind immense dark glasses, I could see that her eyes, too, were brown-black. They had a hurt look to them.

'Never mind the chocolate tart,' Jane Tait said.

'Bittersweet's my favourite.'

'Come on Max, don't play. There are things I need to know.'

I held up my hand, shushing her. 'Another time. Promise.'

I had seen the man.

The woman, in four-inch heels, towered over him in his pale camel-hair wrapround coat, tied loosely with a belt. He stood – or rather scrambled briskly to keep pace with her – about five feet five inches, even in Cuban heels. His thinning hair was carefully combed and held in place against the April breeze by just the right amount of grease.

His sunglasses were smaller than hers, but of the wrap-around kind that hid more of the wearer's face. It didn't matter. I'd know Moe Gordon anywhere, and so would every crook and cop in the Western Hemisphere.

This was my day for celebrities. I'd trailed Jean-Luc Dorani all the way across the Atlantic. But to find Moe Gordon in town at the same time told me the biggies were in motion.

The high rollers of international crime were gathering. I'd come to London at precisely the right moment.

CHAPTER SIX

'Mr Patrick,' the plump man was telling me, 'I have to be brutally frank with you. Your new book is absolute killer dynamite.'

I nodded, hoping that what he was saying warranted a smile. He was an American, this Mr Krochmal, born not too far from either Brooklyn or the Bronx. But fate and perhaps his own talent had landed him on this shore of the Atlantic, in a lovely old suite of offices not far from Piccadilly Circus.

The building in which Fortune Films was housed stood in its own dead-end mews which led back from Old Bond Street along a crooked path until it opened into a courtyard. Someone had planted geraniums and made sure they survived brilliantly in the London air.

It was on to this courtyard, from a height of three floors, that Mr Krochmal's office windows looked down. Or, rather, I looked down, since both Mr Krochmal and Jane Tait were seated at his desk, together with my publisher, Jane Tait's boss, Ian Goodman. I alone stood at the window, trying to salvage what was left of a beautiful April day.

Fortune Films, like its London manager, was American. It had been an English company before the Second World War. When it went broke in 1946 one of the Hollywood giants, using blocked money held in Great Britain, bought Fortune for what everyone invariably referred to in later years as a song.

The song had cost half a million pounds in the days when a pound had been worth a lot. When in time the currency devalued once too often, Hollywood unloaded Fortune to an anonymous group of investors, most of them from the continent, who reduced its scope from producing films to distributing other people's products.

'... and we feel confident that Fortune will make an absolutely dynamite return to the ranks of producing companies with your book as our first vehicle,' Mr Krochmal was explaining to me.

I am as open to flattery as anyone, but there was nothing very rousing about the idea of letting my book serve as a guinea pig to test whether or not Fortune could once again produce pictures.

'Do you have any stars in mind?' I asked, 'any directors?'

'An absolute killer cast,' Krochmal said. 'We're dickering now with Al Pacino for the lead. And we've already signed Rosalind Rue for the role of Ursula.'

I had heard of Al Pacino and I had a fairly good idea what the verb 'to dicker' meant in this case, namely, that he hadn't yet said no. Of Rosalind Rue I knew nothing and was reluctant to confess it.

'What's she done, um, lately?' I asked instead.

'An Oscar nomination last year for supporting actress,' the plump man responded instantly. As I knew about 'dicker' I also knew about 'nomination'. She hadn't got the Oscar but, like so many other actresses, she'd been in the running.

Ian Goodman, my London publisher, glanced at his watch. I had the idea he was beginning to be as bored with this never-never talk as I was. But he surprised me by saying, instead: 'Shouldn't she be here by now?'

Krochmal consulted a very large stainless-steel watch strapped to his wrist by a thick curve of black leather in which more eyelets lived than one could imagine possible. The dial of the watch, in addition to reporting that the time was three o'clock, also conveyed such additional intelligence as the day of the week, the date and, for all I knew, tomorrow's weather. The chubby film man picked up his telephone and muttered something into it, then broke into a smile. 'Right now,' he said and hung up.

With the same shoulder swing that had helped the telephone to its cradle, he continued swivelling his heavy body in its chair until he was facing the door to his office with an expectant look, as if he had reason to believe Santa Claus would be arriving this year in April. The door opened and he was right.

She had removed the sable coat. But the sable hair and the sable eyes gave her away. So did the heart-stopping legs. This time, however, she didn't have on her arm the financial manager for the underground fortunes of all twenty-six US families of organized crime, Moe Gordon.

I glanced at Jane Tait, who had already looked in my direction. 'Max Patrick,' Krochmal said, getting to his feet, 'say hello to a real dynamite lady. Rozzie, this is The Genius himself.'

Her face had the square jaw and high cheekbones of Southern Russia, together with that velvety smooth, faintly olive skin that would never look dry and never wrinkle. At least not for many, many years to come. The hurt look I had seen there before was still there, except when she smiled. She was a woman who seemed to know all about pain. Miss Rue, at a glance, was no older than Jane Tait, turning thirty, but apart from them both being female they seemed to have been assembled on different planets.

This became even more apparent when Jane Tait and her boss stood up. Since I was already on my feet, Miss Rue received what amounted to a standing ovation. She deserved it, if not for the face, which had the same cardiac effect as her legs, then for her gold, openwork, see-through blouse beneath which one almost caught sight – but would never, never be sure – of her nipples. Could I? Couldn't I?

We shook hands and nothing in her welcoming smile

betrayed the goof Krochmal had perpetrated by calling me 'The Genius'.

It happened to be a title that belonged to someone else, for nearly forty years since the Prohibition era. For the foxy way he showed the mobs how to make money and hold on to it, how to evade their taxes and grow fat doing it, Moe Gordon had been called 'The Genius' long before most of us in the room had been born.

Krochmal would probably not know about the nickname, but the actress would. I glanced from her nipples to Jane Tait. Like most tall women, she had breasts which made only a neat convexity in the mauve front of her dress. 'This is my editor, Jane Tait,' I said, 'and my publisher, Ian Goodman.'

We all found seats, even I. There was nothing that great about watching the April sun on the courtyard geraniums, not when Rosalind Rue was within eyeshot.

'I just adore your book,' she began in a low voice that told me nothing about her background except the presence of an expensive voice coach. She had been trained to produce a throaty tone that reverberated in one's inner ear, but no one had had to teach her the right thing to tell an author.

'You've read it, then?' Jane Tait said in that flat British way, not really a question, more of a note of marvel that Miss Rue could read at all.

The actress nodded enthusiastically and kept her smile firmly in place. 'And I'm excited about playing Ursula.'

'You'll need a slight German accent,' I suggested.

'*Natürliche,*' she murmured. 'It will be terribly exciting working with Pacino, too.' She sensed she had overstepped a line. 'Nothing, of course, to the excitement of the story.'

'It's slated as a co-production with a West German company,' the plump producer said then. 'We'll be working in Deutschmarks, which is an absolutely killer currency.'

41

'But the filming will be in the US,' I added in a slightly worried tone. This newest novel, *Licence to Kill*, was a departure for me. I usually set my scenes in foreign countries. This time everything took place in American cities, where the action related specifically to places in each town.

The theme was a fairly gritty one for me, and more technical than usual, having to do with the way an electronics expert made computers pay out large sums of money into his own account, until he ran foul of a mob-controlled conglomerate that put out a hit on him.

When Krochmal failed to respond to my note of anxiety, I added: 'You can't set the story anywhere but the States.'

'We-ell,' he said, and waited. Then: 'Our German money people see it being shot in Frankfurt and Bonn and Dusseldorf. I mean, a city's a city and a computer's a computer. A dynamite story can happen anywhere in the modern business world.'

I glanced first at Jane Tait, then at her boss. 'Well, of course,' Goodman responded abruptly. 'But Fortune must see that we do have to protect our investment in the book. We'll be bringing out the paperback to coincide with the film, naturally, and we don't want the two to look vastly different.'

Krochmal produced a gigantic no-problem shrug. 'They'll look absolutely identical. Guaranteed. Roz's face will be on the book jacket and is anybody gonna complain about that?'

I found myself watching Miss Rue as he delivered this deathless weasel-phrase. Apart from that whisper of pain in her face, it was gorgeously untroubled. No, I thought, nobody ain't gonna complain. Possibly my own face showed that I was still unhappy, however.

'It's early days,' Goodman put in. 'Time enough later to settle everything. Max,' he added warningly, 'we haven't even gone to contract yet.'

It was the eternal voice of the compromiser and the

plump man's soon joined it. 'Everything will be ironed out. No sweat. The important thing is for you, Max, to be happy with Roz and the rest of the cast.'

My eyes had never left hers. Now I smiled slightly – one of those smiles that I am finding it difficult to keep from calling 'rueful' – and said: 'How could anybody be, um, unhappy with Miss Rue?'

This seemed to be the cue Krochmal needed to break up the meeting. He got to his feet in a flurry of 'get-together-next-Wednesday's' and before too many seconds had elapsed Goodman, Jane Tait and I were downstairs in the courtyard, where the dying afternoon sun had turned the geraniums from a fuchsia red to the dark flush of a Sicilian blood-orange.

'Let me give you a lift in my cab,' Goodman was offering.

I shook my head. 'It's not that far to walk.'

'Jane?' he asked.

Her head was shaking, too. 'I've got to check Hatchard's, Ian,' she said. 'Max and I can walk there on his way home.'

We stood for a moment on Old Bond Street watching Goodman's taxi turn the corner towards the Burlington Arcade and disappear in afternoon traffic. Then Jane Tait sighed. 'She really is something, I gather?'

I nodded. 'How good a glimpse of her did you get at lunch in Shepherd Market?'

'Almost as good as your glimpse. I had the idea you were going to inhale her through your eyes and I'd better work fast or there'd be no girl left.'

'You didn't happen to see the man she was with?'

'Short, suntan, late sixties, camel coat, elevator heels, greased-back hair?'

I grinned at her long, solemn face, as she recited from memory. 'You didn't know who he was?'

'I didn't even know who *she* was,' Jane Tait admitted.

I took her arm and we headed through sidestreets towards Piccadilly and the bookshop called Hatchard's.

'But I thought you young, with-it swinging Londoners knew all the celebs.'

'And the globally renowned novelist? You didn't know her either.'

We walked a while in silence. Then she squeezed my arm. 'All of which leads me to wonder just what kind of production Fortune wants to give your book. I'll admit Rosalind Rue is worth looking at, but wouldn't you much rather have looked at Al Pacino in that room?' She walked past Hatchard's bookshop without even a pause.

'Didn't you tell Goodman you—'

She gave me a frown of mock displeasure. 'What is it you American characters always say? Buy me a drink?'

Which was how we found ourselves, a bit later, in the bar lounge at Blue's hotel, off St James's, sipping our second scotch-and-soda. The waiter was old and smooth, like the whisky, and managed to be both efficient and unobtrusive. At the same time he signalled with his eyebrows the message that he quite approved of my taste in female drinking companions.

Although I am partial to drinking with women – editors aside – what was riveting me to my chair as Jane Tait and I sat across a small, polished walnut table from each other was not the fact that she'd made a hit with the waiter.

It was the identical table, two down from ours, where Moe Gordon and Jean-Luc Dorani had been conversing in low voices for the past half hour.

It was just as well that Jane Tait was sitting with her back to the terrifying twosome at the other table. Nor was I about to scare her out of a night's sleep by giving her selected excerpts from the dossiers of these two gentlemen.

Moe Gordon, who looked like everybody's dream of a pussy-cat grandpa, with his whispery voice and cute, soulful eyes, had started life as either a Palermo knife-fighter named Guglielmo Giordano, or an arsonist from

44

Vilna known to the home folks as Motke Grodnovsky. It was a tribute to the power of Moe's money that every trace of him had been wiped out in the old country.

He sprang into history full blown in the early 1920s as a contract killer in the Five Points area of New York, where he worked first for Johnnie Torrio, before the master hood went west to Chicago with Al Capone. Later Moe affiliated with Salvatore Lucania, known more familiarly as Charlie 'Lucky' Luciano.

I watched the pinkie finger of Moe Gordon's right hand curl delicately outward as he sipped his Campari-soda and nodded politely. That nod over the years had sealed many a lucrative deal, from Cuban molasses and rum during Prohibition to total control of the island with Batista as his puppet, from the breaking of a President of the United States to the making of a new one.

The total amount of time Moe Gordon had spent in jail during his long life was, at a wild guess, not more than three months.

Something Jean-Luc Dorani was saying required emphasis. He sat, quietly elegant in a very subdued British Glen Plaid suit. But then he did an un-British thing. He tapped the walnut table with a fingernail even more highly polished than the wood. He tapped it only once, but it shook with the subdued force of the movement. Dorani was like that. On his home turf, in Corsica, where he was said to broker the shipment of every ounce of heroin produced in Europe, the Middle East and Asia, Jean-Luc Dorani had a mansion, a wife, a family and fifty suits hanging in his closets. In Marseilles, his second home, where he had a villa and a mistress, fifty more suits hung neatly in closets. Dorani's cleaning bill alone would have kept a Corsican family eating like royalty.

Many things were said of Jean-Luc Dorani: that he was Moe Gordon's counterpart in Europe, the financial genius who showed the masters of organized crime how to use their money properly, that he was not Corsican at all, but the son of a Hungarian nobleman, one Imre

Dohranyi, a famous forger of pre-war Europe, that his father had, in fact, been a Corsican bandit who had raped a Sicilian princess and then stolen the baby from her.

As Jane Tait and I finished our third drink, this fine example either of twisted ancestry or vile rumourmongering arose, shook hands coolly with Moe Gordon, and left the bar lounge. We chatted idly, she trying to work the conversation around to her suspicions of lunchtime, when she had called me an international crook. After three drinks, however, she found it impossible to keep her mind on anything for longer than a minute or two.

A man stood in the far doorway and looked around the lounge until his glance fastened on Moe Gordon. He approached with an almost deferential slink, somewhat like a head waiter being summoned by a Rockefeller to remove a plate of bad oysters.

He stood for a moment at Gordon's elbow, muttering something. The elderly man gave him a sharp look and indicated the chair Dorani had recently vacated.

Unlike the two master thieves whose dossiers I had been fancifully piecing together, the man who now sat down was totally known to me. Dave Greeley was his name. He stood about my height, but much thinner, with small eyes set just a millimetre too close. I had known him first in Korea, where he'd been a fellow Intelligence officer. Later he'd drifted into the CIA and done so badly that even that refuge for the inept eventually terminated his service.

He was now, I had reason to believe, something like an assistant vice president, or assistant cashier of one of the big US banks in London.

I had no idea why a Dave Greeley knew a Moe Gordon well enough to sit and chat with him. That Gordon and other mob figures had lines into the CIA is well known. Perhaps Greeley had served as liaison. Nor did I know how a junior officer of a large bank branch could justify a public meeting with a mobster of Gordon's calibre. Perhaps Moe Gordon had his savings in —

I sat up straighter in my chair. 'Let's go,' I whispered to Jane Tait.

In the lobby I excused myself for a moment and went to the reception desk. I hadn't liked the way Dorani had walked out. Too final. Had my transatlantic bird flown for good?

'The gentleman in the Glen Plaid who's staying here,' I murmured to the clerk. 'Can I leave a message for him in his box?'

'Mr Dorani's not —' He stopped, discretion getting the better of him for a moment. Then: 'At this time, he is not a guest with us, sir.'

'I see.'

I returned to the lobby and started the business of sending Jane Tait on her way. 'Well,' I said heartily, 'see you tomorrow, then?'

'Can I see what kind of suite they've given you?' She punched the 'Up' button for the elevator.

I frowned at her. She was behaving very un-Jane-Tait-like. I had a smallish suite, as it happened, because this wasn't my usual hotel. I'd booked in hurriedly without a reservation and all they'd been able to give me was a room with a bed alcove at one end and a rather attractive living area at the other. There was a refrigerator, towards which Jane Tait made a beeline.

Once she'd made us drinks, she settled down across from the sofa I was sitting on and removed her strapped shoes. She crossed her long legs. She had narrow feet. Then she switched on some music. A samba softly pulsed through the room. She clicked off one light. We watched each other in a sort of intimate dusk.

A few moments ago, downstairs, I had a sudden blinding insight into what had brought Gordon, Dorani and Brother Dave Greeley together. I needed to think about it. Alone. But Jane Tait had other ideas.

'Look,' she said, 'Miss Rue isn't here. But I am.' She came over to the sofa. It was only a moment before Jane Tait had my undivided attention.

CHAPTER SEVEN

I woke only once, at four a.m. Normally I'm not one of these where-am-I people. I know what bed I'm in. But the body beside me was unfamiliar and, for a moment, I had trouble remembering I was in London.

Jane Tait slept soundly. She had turned out to be one of those who sleep *into* a bed, her long, slim body seemingly swallowed up by the linens, her head half buried in the pillow.

In the dim light I sat up on one elbow and watched her for a time, wondering whether, in fact, I had thoughtlessly fucked up my publishing arrangements in Great Britain. Clearly Jane Tait was no longer just my editor. Of course, a lot depended on what happened between us when she awoke.

I slipped out of bed and padded over to the sofa where the whole unthinking experiment had begun. I snapped on a small sidetable light and began leafing through the assortment of newspapers I had bought yesterday in the vain hope of reading them before getting to bed last night. Jet lag kept my internal clock out of kilter.

The one thing I clearly remembered, before whisky and propinquity had contrived to do in Jane Tait and me, was a startling aperçu that had arrived, reeking of malt fumes, when I observed Dave Greeley, of the Manhattan Bank and Trust, Mayfair Branch, chatting with Moe Gordon, of the National Crime Syndicate, for all the world like banker and customer.

That had been it, of course. Gordon was probably Greeley's best customer. If I knew how Moe Gordon's mind worked – an assumption of total hubris on my part – he would have not one but several accounts in his bank, all of them what the English call 'external', meaning they belonged to people who were not UK subjects and did not live in the UK.

All sorts of perks attend the external account, but none so valuable as the fact that the bank is not required to report the ins and outs of the account to Inland Revenue, the English counterpart of our Internal Revenue.

The two IR's speak to each other, not only regularly, but persistently. The fiscal doings of American residents of England are reported with the speed of light to their home tax-collecting agency. Unless they are entitled to have an external account.

I imagined Moe Gordon would have as many as he was entitled to, and perhaps a few safe-deposit boxes as well. What all this had to do with Jean-Luc Dorani was not yet clear. Furthermore, a customer of Moe Gordon's stature would speak only to the manager himself. Why was he conducting his business with a miserable subordinate like Dave Greeley?

My thoughts flickered in and out of the problem while I paged through the pink pages of the London *Financial Times*. Then I scanned the Paris *Herald-Tribune* and *The Guardian*.

The news was a day old coming from the States. I already knew, for example, that the recently elected Presidential administration, which had sought and got its vote on the basis of being everything to everyone, was now deep in all the serious trouble that had been predicted for it.

The flexibility seemed to have drained out of the US economy. Profits were down. Unemployment was up. Businessmen in search of capital found lenders unwilling to risk money on such an iffy proposition as capitalism. While the value of the dollar flickered up and down on world currency market, at home its purchasing power sank regularly. Inflation grew steadily worse.

All of these grave matters had been true before the election, of course, but some had been smothered in mindless optimism and others, like the unemployment rate, had been concealed by carefully fudging the figures. It now appeared, for example, that the government's figures had been showing a levelling rate of joblessness because each month, by federal fiat, hundreds of thousands of unemployed were removed, statistically, from the labour market.

If a person had been out of work for a year or eighteen months, the government told itself, he or she was obviously no longer looking for work. Off the rolls came such people. It was marvellous how many jobless could be made to disappear from the statistical reports in this fashion.

The mood of unrest in the States, as I knew from my own experience, now borne out by ashen-faced articles in the European press, was coming from an unexpected quarter. The blacks had long been feared as the focus of future rioting and revolt. Students had for a time been viewed in the same light.

But nobody imagined that the conservative, beer-drinking working class, which still believed in the American Dream, would desert its TV screen long enough to turn ugly. These folks had stood still for every imaginable insult, including the crowning one of seeing their man, Nixon, make the American Dream come true, thus exposing it.

They had watched their savings disappear, then their wages, then their jobs. Their homes went next, which meant their cars and their television sets. It was at that point that the rioting began in widely separate areas like Buffalo, New York, and Redlands, California. Windows were smashed in banks. Supermarkets were looted and trashed. Used-car lots were raided and, to give the booty a high-octane guzzle, gasoline stations were seized.

There was no politics to the movement. It wasn't a movement yet, because there were no leaders, just a few blue-collar and hard-hat workers and their wives who had discussed it and decided they'd had enough. Nor was there, as yet, enough momentum or mass to worry official law-enforcement spokesmen.

But if the States were heading towards a smash-up, Western Europe looked even worse, if one relied solely on the newspapers. The rising strength of the French and Italian Left, mainly Communist parties liberated from Moscow control, gave heart to the Left everywhere in Spain, Portugal, Greece, Scandinavia, the Low Countries, even in ever-more-prosperous West Germany.

Coalitions with Socialists and Social Democrats, spurned in the past, now became overnight realities. Local and regional elections went Left. By autumn – when through a dangerous coincidence France, Italy and three smaller countries would be holding general elections – the steady advance of the Left was expected to consolidate into legal control mandated by the voting masses.

If one could believe the *Financial Times* columnist, European business and financial managers had begun to feel trapped. There was only so much investment Switzerland would absorb; she had already closed her borders to more.

There was no point in looking across the Atlantic for investment opportunities. Other fields were as scorched as one's own. The columnist likened the feeling of western capitalist leaders to that of a rat whose every effort to solve the maze has failed.

'Behavioural scientists,' he wrote, 'tell us that such rats, frustrated beyond the norm, turn passive, apathetic, catatonic. They do not respond to stimuli and, after a while, they sicken and die.'

I pondered for only a moment the idea of rat-catatonia, but dismissed it as unworthy of the gravity of the situation. More than one newspaper now asked the same question: had Karl Marx been right a hundred years ago when he'd predicted the decline, crisis and fall of capitalism? We'd always called him wrong; was only his time-table at fault?

But I knew something even the awesomely erudite *Financial Times* columnist didn't. He knew all about the legitimate business establishment. I knew about organized crime.

I knew that while the shoot-the-bastards techniques of early freebooting capitalists had long died out, in one sector of the business world they were still alive. Only one major conglomerate – albeit perhaps the single most profitable one in the world – still regularly resorted to the garrote, the knife, the gun, the bomb and many more lethal methods of business persuasion.

Its chief American financial officer was huddling in London with its principal European money manager.

Around five a.m., my eyelids began to lower again. I crawled back into bed without disturbing Jane Tait. Around six I awakened slightly when she rolled over on top of me. Hazily, we did pleasant things to each other. I dropped off again and slept so soundly that when I awoke the room was flooded with brilliant morning sunshine.

I glanced at my watch. Nine a.m. I glanced at my partner. She had vanished. A note had been propped up against my telephone.

'Ad conference for new posters on *Licence to Kill* at eleven this morning. Please be there to help me hold the art department at bay. Yr. obed'nt editor, E. J. Tait.'

I sighed with relief. So *that* was all right.

CHAPTER EIGHT

At eleven o'clock Jane Tait was fighting her art department by herself. I had taken a leisurely shower and shave, set aside my travelled-in clothes for the valet and put through a telephone call to a Londoner named Jack Philemon.

As nearly as I could tell, I'd wakened him by the call. 'Care to take a stroll around Soho with me?'

'Oaiou,' he moaned. Jack had taken a history honours at Oxford, I believe. He had for some years now supported his taste for expensive rare books by working, when he had to, as a private investigator for very private clients. Like me.

'I need to pick up something, um, unusual in the way of electronic devices,' I explained.

'Wanna go shoppy-shoppy, sweetums?' Jack's morning humour is nothing worth reporting in full detail. We set a date to meet at a shop in Beak Street in Soho. I got there first and waited a while in the pleasant April sunshine until I spotted Jack coming along the street. He was easy.

He is slighter than I am, and possibly five years younger, say early thirties. But he has a highly visible mass of red hair so bright I've often been tempted to ask him what dye he used on it. Jack has the true redhead's fair complexion, thin, pink with a faint undertinge of green, that shows every ray of sun in the form of large, splotched freckles.

'No charge for this one,' Jack said by way of greeting. 'On the house.'

'So kind,' I murmured sarcastically. Normally Jack's daily fee started at a hundred pounds. It guaranteed a client not only total concentration, but total privacy. If anyone as eccentric as Jack can be lovable, this was his most attractive virtue: he forgot all about a client the moment the job was done.

I had hoped to buy the Mitsui 6001, a small black thingie no bigger than a large liquorice gumdrop, with a mercury cell battery, a life of one month and a transmitting radius of two hundred metres. None of the speciality electronics shops had any, although one man offered to order it for me on sixty-day delivery.

Jack convinced me to settle for one of the Uher devices, a bit larger, but also more sensitive. It had the added advantage of some sort of stickum along one side of what looked like a small matchbox, the kind posh restaurants give away. One removed the covering sheet from the stickum and the device could be secured in almost any out-of-the-way spot. Total price £150. I said I'd be back.

At the corner of Beak Street and Regent Street, I stopped and shook Jack's hand. 'As far as you go for now, Jack.'

'Paranoid bah-stid.' His greenish eyes watched me. 'More later?'

'Likely.'

He walked off in the direction of Oxford Street. I made sure he was out of sight before continuing to my own destination. I trust Jack, but only when I absolutely must.

I walked by way of Regent and Brook Streets towards Grosvenor Square and the main branch office of Manhattan Bank and Trust. As I stood at the counter, changing some dollars into sterling, I glanced idly at the officers seated in the rear. None of them remotely resembled Dave Greeley.

'Isn't Mr Greeley in this morning?' I asked the teller.

'He's downstairs in Safe Deposit, sir. The steps are there.'

I nodded, took my stack of ten-pound notes and left in the direction of the stairs, but veered off and left the bank first. I stood for a moment on the steps outside and stared at the Square in the throes of spring. It was a pleasant sight.

Aside from the FDR Memorial, the other note of interest in Grosvenor Square was a flock of newly arrived robins, scraggy and thin from a hard winter, who bobbed up and down over the pale new grass to pull forth tasty elevenses in the form of worms.

I turned back in the direction of Beak Street, passing the Stars and Stripes as they fluttered from the façade of the American Embassy. It was, in fact, the next building to the Manhattan Bank, which was located on a street just off the square.

The Beak Street man was kind enough to test the nicad battery for me and demonstrate how to switch on the device. He accepted my £150 and bade me God-speed, little knowing or caring where I was about to plant the Uher. I had, in fact, mumbled something about 'checking up on the little woman', which made any crime I committed one of, um, passion.

Back in Grosvenor Square, more robins had joined the diet of worms. I entered the bank and walked downstairs to Safe Deposit. There he sat, a human worm in his own little hole, Dave Greeley, keeper of the vaults.

I stood outside the locked Herculite glass doors and rapped on them with a ten-penny piece. He looked up, blinked, got to his feet, fumbled for his keys and had the door open before the stupid son-of-a-bitch recognized me.

'Paul!' he exclaimed, pulling back as if stung. 'Hey, there, good buddy!' He had known me in Korea as Lt Paul Maxwell, of which name only a lonely Max remained. Oh, what a tangled web we weave when first we practise to deceive.

'Dave, for Christ's sake.' I pumped his hand as I glanced around the room.

This area was devoted to servicing customers, I gathered. After they'd visited the vault and got their box, they could return here to a small private room with a lockable door where they might sit in privacy and play with their gold coins or diamonds or whatever they kept in their lock boxes.

'Hey, Paul,' Dave demanded. 'What're you up to, good buddy?'

'I had no idea you still worked here,' I replied, dodging the issue. 'You're just the man I'm looking for.'

My glance wandered around the Safe Deposit area as we talked. It had the general appearance of an oversized tunnel and had obviously once been the vault of a much older structure on which the modern bank building now rested.

The tunnel extended in the direction of Soho about two hundred metres, its walls lined with the small velvety-steel doors of safe deposit box receptacles, each with two brass inserts for keys. At the far end of the tunnel an impressive Diebold vault door stood open, its time-release mechanism glittering in the bright overhead lights.

'Looking to open a box, good buddy?'

I had been, but I didn't want Greeley knowing my Max Patrick name. That wasn't it, either. I didn't mind him knowing; after all my face was on the book dust-jacket. But I didn't want him being able to prove I had rented a safe deposit box under what he knew to be a pseudonym.

That bit of information gave him too much leverage. I was certain there was some sort of law against taking out a box in an assumed name. It was one of those laws no one pays any attention to unless one is a stupid, greedy little worm like Dave Greeley.

'I'm in town a while,' I said, 'and my hotel safe is a joke.' I moved past him down the corridor, examining the various sizes of the lock-box doors.

'Our rates are the best in London,' Greeley informed me.

My glance shot towards the ceiling of the tunnel where a thick electrical conduit connected each lighting fixture. 'What about the vault? Storage there, too?'

He moved ahead of me now, leading the way. 'This is our maximum security area,' he bragged. I found myself wondering how secure any of this was if the custodian let in good buddies at will. Who else did he let in besides me? And with how few precautions?

We were inside the vault now. The walls were lined with much larger lock-box doors, easily the size of those lockers at airports. I had no idea who saved what in these super-safe hideaways, but chances were that well-to-do Americans kept cash, jewellery and securities here.

'What's that gizmo?' I asked, pointing to a small grey box on the inside of the vault over the entrance. I knew what it was. The idea was to distract good buddy Dave while I switched on the Uher device.

'Marvel of electronics,' he explained. 'Three thousand pounds sterling of marvels. When I close the vault door at three p.m. it gives me five minutes to get the hell out. Then, anybody makes a noise in that vault and bells go off all over town. It's so sensitive it damned near picks up the noise a spider makes spinning a web.' He cackled foolishly.

'Look at the stonework,' I said next, pointing to the far wall where the large individual chunks of dressed lime-stone were seemingly fitted together without mortar.

'That would be the foundation wall itself,' Dave said. 'It's about a century old, at least.' He ran his finger along the horizontal joint between two stones.

Behind him, I stripped the release-sheet from the sticky side of the Uher. 'I imagine there's a premium rate on these lock boxes,' I guessed.

'Well, it does go by size,' he admitted, moving past me

to the entrance. 'And the additional security.' He patted the time-release mechanism behind its tempered-glass window.

As he turned to lead the way out of the vault, I reached up as high over the entrance as I could and struck the Uher on top of the electronic sensor box in an area of shadow where it might not be noticed for a while. I docilely followed Dave Greeley out of the vault and along the corridor to his desk.

'Looks good,' I said then. 'I'll be back in a few days to, um, sign the papers, okay?'

'Can do, good buddy,' he assured me. Then, unwilling to let me go that fast, he took my arm. 'What's shaking with the old gang?'

'Beats the shit out of me.'

'I don't mean Photo Recon,' he said then, his voice dropping to a discreet murmur, 'I mean, you know, The Outfit.'

I gave him a pained frown. 'Dave, you know I was never in The, um, Outfit.'

'Shit you wasn't, good buddy.'

I shook my head. He'd been hurt when the CIA had let him go. He'd peopled his memory with all sorts of good-buddy associations, building up an imaginary pantheon of friends, all of whom were 'in' while he was 'out'. They had a name for his trouble – not paranoia, but something like it.

'Have it your way,' I said at last. 'See you in a day or so.'

He let my arm go and opened the heavy glass doors. He was still standing there behind them, watching wistfully as I climbed halfway up the stairs and looked back down at him. He smiled tentatively and waved. The stairs turned then and he was lost to sight.

Outside, the noon sun was pleasingly warm. I glanced into the next block of buildings and found myself looking at my publisher's offices. Perfect location. I would get Jane Tait to have them assign me a small office overlooking the Square, at least for a few weeks while I did 're-search' or whatever excuse made sense. I would install the FM receiver in that office.

The distance from my publisher's to the Uher device stuck inside the vault of Manhattan Bank and Trust Company was about 500 metres. And the man who'd sold me the Uher had guaranteed its range for more than that.

Now it was just a matter of timing and luck.

CHAPTER NINE

I began to see that Jane Tait had been right when she told me, on my first day in London, that the successful writer has entrée everywhere. At my publisher's they apparently routed some shadowy sub-editor out of a cubbyhole on the fourth floor of their building. The room was perfect for my research work. It had, in fact, a clear view of the façade of the Manhattan Bank and Trust branch and, for patriotic fervour, also gave me a stirring sight of Old Glory flapping each day over the US Embassy.

My research materials were simple enough: a small FM receiver whose tuner was permanently fixed at the wavelength of the tiny Uher microphone-transmitter I had stuck to the roof of the bank vault, a notebook and several novels. I was about to add a miniature tape recorder but it proved unnecessary. My bug wasn't producing anything worth recording.

God, but I learned more than anyone would ever want to know about the daily routine of David Bushnell Greeley. It was like being married to him and, at the same time, marooned with him on a desert island.

My publisher's people, Jane Tait included, left me entirely alone, except for an occasional note slipped under the door of my cubbyhole. And the Greeleyana reeled on. He hummed, did Dave. He also broke wind now and then, producing after lunch a long, controlled belch, a marvel of hydraulic engineering.

He paced a lot during the day and did a lot of heavy sighing, too. Flatulence aside, the pacing and sighing were clear evidence either of tension, depression or both.

I hadn't yet got a clue as to why.

I did get snatches of conversation with the ten or twelve customers who came in each morning and afternoon. I had timed Greeley's lunch hour the first day and took pains to match mine to his, running any errands along the way.

It was a dull life, but not as bad as one might have expected, since the Safe Deposit vaults were only open the six hours from nine-thirty to three-thirty, and I snatched a free hour when Dave left to feed. I managed to get through *Moby Dick* again, a two-day job, and also to enjoy the latest of Gore Vidal's fanciful re-creations of American history.

By the third day, I had Greeley's routine so memorized that there were no surprises left. I toyed with the idea of handing over the surveillance to Jack Philemon, but decided against it. Dave's only personal business was a call he always made near quitting time, to someone called Clarissa. This was a regular event, although it was clear that Clarissa was not a wife. Not his, at any rate.

I had finished Vidal and was starting the new Updike novel – and finding it heavy going through its overlay of, um, right-wing cant – when, on the morning of the fourth day, the routine was shattered.

The telephone rang in Greeley's vault at about eleven a.m. 'Safe Deposit, Greeley speaking,' he answered.

There was a pause and then the silly ass produced the start of one of life's more fatuous lines. 'I've told you never to ca—' But his caller cut him off by saying something rather sharply, because Greeley's next words were spoken in a contrite tone.

'Oh, I see. Yes, of course.'

There was another pause as he listened. 'Yes,' he said at last. 'I know the place. Fulham Road, isn't it?' More listening. 'A few doors down from San Frediano's. Oh, that late?' Another pause. 'I'll have to ask my relief if he minds trading lunch hours with me.'

He listened for only a short while, then said 'Right'

and hung up. Pacing. Heavy sigh. Another. He seemed
to be having trouble with his breathing. Sound of a telephone being dialled.

'Canby, would you mind trading lunch hours with
me?' Canby proved willing. The pacing continued but
the sighing stopped. All was well, and Greeley would be
able to keep his late-notice lunch date. I wondered if I
ought to keep it with him.

My hour away from the boring cubbyhole and the
FM receiver was precious to me, however. I had things to
do with the time. Moreover, lunch was probably with
the mysterious Clarissa, who seemed to be able to get
good buddy Dave to do whatever she wished of him.

I saw him leave the bank at five minutes to one p.m.,
hail a cab and leave for his appointment. I quit the premises, but got back at the stroke of two in time to overhead Greeley's return.

'Everything okay, Dave?' Canby's voice asked.

'Fine.' Muffled tone.

'I'm for upstairs then.'

'Good-o. Thanks.'

Everything wasn't okay, Dave. The voice, for one
thing. Perhaps Clarissa had given him the gate. Perhaps
he'd eaten a bad lunch. His voice was slower and vaguely
softer than I remembered it.

Although lunch was over, there were no spectacular
reports from either end of Dave Greeley, nor was he
pacing. In fact, he was the quietest Dave Greeley I could
remember listening to. The few customers who arrived
in the hour of business time left were greeted politely
but not by name.

I decided to take a look at Dave Greeley before the
vaults closed.

It was three-twenty-nine p.m. when I rapped on his
glass door with my coin. He glanced up, frowned, came to
the door and opened it. 'Yes?'

I frowned back. He had Dave's height and thinness,
his piggy eyes, too, set a shade too close. He had the

cadaverous look as well. 'I want to rent a box,' I said.

His frown deepened. 'Too late now, mate,' he said in a creditable American accent. Except that I wasn't Dave's mate, I was his good buddy. For all his years in England, he'd apparently never picked up the 'mate' thing. Until now.

'It's just half past three,' I persisted. 'They let me in upstairs.'

'No lookout of mine. My books,' he added in a tougher tone, 'are closed for the day. Open again Monday morning. There you go.'

I stepped back and let him lock the door in my face. It had been quite a lunch for David Bushnell Greeley. He'd come back a whole new man.

When I got out on the street I hailed a taxi and gave him San Frediano's address on the Fulham Road. Known to its regulars as Sanfred's, the place was a favourite of mine. Life would have been easier for me if Dave Greeley had gone there, rather than somewhere nearby. At Sanfred's they would answer my questions.

Halting the cab, but staying inside, I surveyed the street in both directions from San Frediano's only to decide that there were too many possibilities. I really didn't want to stir up anybody by asking a lot of questions in a lot of places and describing Dave in all of them. I wasn't ready to surface yet in this affair, not without knowing what the hell it was all about.

'Take me to Blue's Hotel. Know it?'

'Off S'n Jymses, eyn it?'

'Right.'

What with Friday afternoon traffic, we didn't get back to my hotel until after half past four. Which was why I came upon Rosalind Rue. Not in the bar. Not in the lobby. In my room.

News item, Acapulco *Prensa del Pacifica,* 20 December:

Want to know where potential presidential hopefuls go to stock up on sun before tackling a grueling set of February primaries? One Democratic front-runner is the current guest of entertainer Paul Sedotti, who's borrowed the magnificent Moe Gordon manse for the Christmas season. Paul's asked Roz Rue to be hostess for a round of partying.

CHAPTER TEN

It didn't startle her at all to have me walk in and catch her between the king-sized bed and the long, low chest of drawers. As a matter of fact, she only looked up for a moment and continued with what I had caught her doing.

Folding and putting away my shirts.

I stood there for a long while, watching her. She had given up the see-through blouse in which I'd first met her and was wearing instead a kind of fluttery chiffon top and slacks that flared loosely only around her calves. The rest of her as she bent away from me to put the last of the shirts away was outlined as distinctly as any anatomist could wish.

Her hair, which was long and black, lay in thick, loose curls and seemed to have a languorous life of its own, moving just a beat behind the rest of her head motion, as if wanting to prolong the delicious feeling.

'Domestic scene,' I finally said.

She straightened up as she turned towards me. It was impossible not to admire the calculated series of movements which brought her breasts up and thrusting forward through the thin material of the blouse.

'Do you mind?' she asked then, letting her hurt look show a little.

This kind of question, from a beautiful woman discovered in one's bedroom, is almost impossible to answer. 'Should I?'

'Well it's a bit ... what do they call it over here? Cheeky?'

'That's what they call it.'

'I've been phoning you since we met and you're never here.'

'You didn't leave messages.'

'I don't,' she explained, mysteriously.

It seemed clear this was all the explanation she was going to produce. 'Thank you for putting away my things. I'm afraid the room was in a mess.'

'The valet had left little laundry packages here and there,' she said. 'I thought you wouldn't mind me neatening things.'

'How did you —'

'Get in?' she finished for me. 'I told the chambermaid you were expecting me for drinks and had asked me to wait in your suite. My own's just down the hall.'

I started for the tiny refrigerator. 'Drink?'

'I —'

'Just to make your story good if the maid bursts in on us.'

She laughed softly and, in a swish of wide slacks, rear end twitching tightly in its casing, she moved to the self-same sofa from which Jane Tait had managed the seduction of Max Patrick three – or had it been four – nights before. The piece of furniture seemed destined to play a role in my London life.

'No ice,' she said, as I poured some whisky into two glasses. 'Touch of soda.'

I handed her drink over and took care to sit across the low cocktail table from the sofa. We lifted our drinks to each other, silently, and then sipped for a moment. 'Do you make your home in New York?' I asked in my best formal manner, 'or the Coast?'

'Both. I'm a New York girl, of course.'

'Born there?'

'Is anyone? New Orleans.'

'No sign of it in your speech.'

'Southern accent?' she asked. 'But the New Orleans accent isn't really Southern. And, then, there were all those speech courses.'

'At Tulane?'

She shook her head. 'I left for New York long before college. Changed my name en route.'

'From what?'

'It's Rouilly,' she said, making a dipthong of it and then spelling it. 'Really Rouilly.' She produced that soft laugh again. It reverberated somewhere inside my head. As long as she smiled one could forget the pain in her face. 'Originally it was Russian. Grandpa fled to Paris and took a very French name. We pronounced it the French way, instead of Ruly or Rowly. So it wouldn't work any other way than Rue.'

'For remembrance? Or is that rosemary?'

'She wore her rue with a difference. I, believe it or not, did Ophelia in high school. It's not much of a part.'

'Then you're a stage actress, originally.'

She sipped her drink in an experimental fashion, as if planning to write a critique of it later. 'I've done the whole thing. Do-wah chorus singing on Dionne Warwick recordings. Two years of soap opera. Toilet tissue commercials for TV. Off Broadway Ibsen. Off-Off Broadway soft porn. Regional theatre in Dallas and Minneapolis. Industrial films. Voice-over narration for psoriasis ads. Summer theatre at Williamstown. Book clerk in Brentano's two summers in a row.' She paused and pointed a finger at me. 'That's where I became a Max Patrick fan.'

She delivered the line with just the right throwaway sincerity. I smiled pleasantly. 'Bullshit,' I said.

For some reason this caused her to double over with quiet laughter. When she got hold of herself she stared for a moment at her drink and then took a hefty slug of it instead of the scientific sample-sips she'd been demonstrating before.

'Only the part about being a fan of yours,' she confessed then. 'The rest of my history is true.'

'You left out the Hollywood part.'

She shrugged. I can never express my full appreciation

67

for what a beautiful woman with beautiful breasts can do with a simple shrug. 'It's the usual story, Max. You've probably written it a few times yourself.'

'Um, let me think.' I let some dead air go by, not because I didn't know what came next, but because I wasn't sure I ought to come on that knowledgeably with her. I decided we'd progressed beyond the point of playing I-never-knew-that games.'

'There was a cast party,' I said then. 'Or a double date set up by another actress in the play. Your date was a businessman. Older. Just in town for a week or so.' I stopped to watch her, but her lovely, square-jawed face, with its soft hollows under high cheekbones, was totally expressionless.

'His moves weren't gross,' I went on. 'They had finesse. He had fallen for you. He had business interests on the Coast. There was a first-class airline ticket for you and the clincher was that he'd made it round-trip. Nothing crass.' I paused again. Something in her face had darkened slightly, but the blank look remained.

'The next part isn't clear to me,' I continued, 'Malibu beach cottage? Apartment on Sunset, where it runs into Beverly Hills? At any rate, auditions, not too many of them, but for film people you'd heard of. No jobs but lots of exposure at parties. He'd arranged for a really top agent to represent you. He wasn't always on the Coast. A life like that gets lonely.'

'No one to talk with,' she quoted, without singing the words, 'I'm by myself. No one to walk with but I'm happy on the shelf.'

Her voice sounded haunted. She had stopped looking at me and was staring into her drink. All the hurt showed now, openly. 'I didn't get a job in flicks for a year. One solid year.'

During which you stayed dutifully on the shelf, I added silently. The temptations were tremendous, I guessed, but there was probably no one out there who didn't know she was private property. Nobody in the business would have made a move towards her.

The silence in my hotel room had gathered for some moments now. Rosalind Rue seemed mesmerized by her drink, gazing darkly into its depths as if in such an amber crystal she could read not only her past but her future.

'Did you know him then as, um, Moe Gordon?' I asked.

She blinked. She did blink. It broke the spell. She looked up at me. 'Max,' she said then, 'I need that part in your book.'

I sat up straighter in my chair. 'Fortune hasn't even bought it yet.'

'They will. They like it. I'd heard about *Licence to Kill* back in the States. Apparently it's based on a real happening?'

I never blink, not under that sort of surprise pressure. But it was something of a shock to learn that the boys recognized their own scam, even in fictional form. Since none of it had ever got in the American newspapers, they had probably wondered how I came by such accurate details.

'Who told you that? Moe?'

She shook her head. 'Being his friend has certain disadvantages. I'm alone a lot, and even when we're together I don't understand half the things he says. When we're having drinks or dinner with people, I understand even less.'

'But it has one major advantage,' I pointed out. 'You don't have to ask a poor hard-working novelist for the female lead in a film. You only have to ask the man who owns Fortune.'

'Implying that Moe owns it?'

'Moe and Company.'

'If you think that's a plus,' she said darkly, 'you don't know show business.' She finished the rest of her drink and handed it back to me for a refill. 'What would Krochmal look like as a creative person if he let his money men dictate who played what role? That sort of thing went out with the custard pie. And he has to attract a top director. What director would let a backer tell him who to cast? There are egos here of the giant, family size.' She watched me make her a fresh drink. Her face seemed even more unhappy.

I gave her the drink. 'Cheer up.'

She frowned at her glass as if I'd managed to include a housefly in it. 'Max, if I'm ever going to graduate from kept woman to movie star, I have to do it myself. On my own. And, perhaps ...' her voice went a shade lower, '... with your help?'

Not her words, but the timbre of them, had begun to scramble my brains ever so slightly, kind of an ultrasonic experience, not at all unpleasant but disconcerting.

'Roz,' I began, 'let me acquaint you with your, um, unique powers. You are not the girlfriend of just any rich old codger. Your particular codger is a man whose slightest wish is law. He's probably never shown you that side of him because if you realized how much raw power he wields, you'd start demanding a lot more from him than he's had to give. He wants to keep your relationship uncluttered by violent attacks of the gimmes.'

'He's told me a dozen times he doesn't interfere in the operations he controls.'

'That's nonsense. When Moe Gordon itches, there isn't an employee of his who doesn't start scratching.'

'I've never even heard him issue an order.'

'He wouldn't in front of witnesses.'

'I'm not exactly a wi —'

'For Moe the world is filled with witnesses.' I glanced down at my own drink and saw that it was still full. 'Furthermore, men like Moe Gordon don't have to issue orders. Their underlings know exactly what's demanded of them. In fact, the worst trouble Gordon gets into is when an eager-beaver stooge over-achieves because he thinks he's making points with the boss.'

She nodded glumly, as if she'd seen evidence of this

herself. 'Do you have a dinner engagement?' she asked then.

I leaned back in my chair. As a matter of fact, I didn't. If I'd had one it might have been with Jane Tait. That would have been a logical extension of either our professional relationship or the new personal one. But Jane Tait had been cooling it. All week only a note under the door of my cubbyhole. Strictly business, as if she wanted me to know that we both understood the nature of a one-night stand.

'No,' I admitted. 'But surely you do.'

'He's left London for the weekend.'

'This town dies on weekends. Everyone's in the country. It's like Manhattan. Where's he gone?'

She sipped whisky in her original experimental style. 'The continent.' She glanced anxiously at me. 'Don't you drink?'

I lifted my glass. 'Your conversation's been so fascinating ...' There was something I had to ask and it was going to be embarrassing not only to her but, in a way, to me. 'Roz, is there some sort of bodyguard who floats around in the background?'

'Two of them.'

'Where are they this weekend?'

'With him. I think.'

'He trusts you alone in London?'

She stared at me for a long moment. Then she put down her drink and got up. She moved slowly around the edge of the cocktail table until she was standing in front of me. She was not a tall woman. Jane Tait was a tall woman. If Jane Tait had been standing there in slacks, I would have been staring at her belt buckle. As it was, I was looking into Rosalind Rue's cleavage.

'I'm not married to him,' she said in her low voice. Her smile erased the pain in her face. Her words tickled at my inner ear. As if to block their effect, she took my head in her hands and nestled it between her breasts.

CHAPTER ELEVEN

It had not been an easy night, nor a restful one. We did something to each other, Rosalind and I, that kept both of us on edge. It may have been simple sexual tension that made it unthinkable to sleep. I'd like to believe that, and the not-unpleasant ache in my groin was a memento of sorts, but not of a peaceful night.

I was asleep, finally, at about ten a.m. when the telephone rang. My eyes jumped open. I turned and saw that she was still asleep beside me. I grabbed the telephone before the switchboard operator downstairs tried a second ring.

'Yes?'

'Good morning,' Jane Tait said. 'Oh, Christ, Max, don't tell me I woke you?'

'Yes.'

I was watching Rosalind's face. In repose, dead asleep, there was no sign of that darker note of pain. She seemed at peace.

'I'm having people over tonight for drinks and dinner,' Jane Tait went on. 'Can you make it?'

Rosalind's eyes were fluttering open. She stared at me for a long moment before she realized I was on the telephone.

'Hello?' Jane Tait's voice came through the receiver clearly.

'Yes.'

'Yes, what, Max? Yes you're still there or yes you can come tonight?'

I gestured with the telephone, in a what-do-you-think

movement. Rosalind shrugged sleepily. It was an even prettier movement lying on her back than standing up. 'I don't know, Jane,' I said then. 'Am I to be your date or something?'

'Not at all.' She sounded irritated. 'The party's been on the books for weeks now and there's already a friend playing host.'

'Mixing drinks? That sort of drill?'

'Max, can you give me an answer please?' She seemed to be trying to keep her temper. 'If you come I'll pull in another girl to even things up.'

'If I come may I bring my own?'

There was a short silence at Jane Tait's end of the conversation. Then: 'By all means.' Crisp. Civil.

'Then the answer's yes.'

'Marvellous,' she said. Another silence, a bit longer. 'Is it Miss Rue?'

Rosalind could, of course, hear Jane's voice almost as well as I. I gave her a look of wide-eyed astonishment across the pillows. 'You're clairvoyant.'

'She's there right now, isn't she?' Jane Tait pounced.

'Come on, Jane.'

'On the side of the bed away from the telephone,' my darling editor said. 'Max, by all means bring her tonight. I wouldn't miss this for the world. Seven o'clock.'

'Miss what?' I asked, but she'd hung up.

Neither Rosalind nor I had much to say for a while. Then, in a lazy murmur that even now had the power to make my inner ear tingle, she said: 'The lady is pissed off.'

'Possibly.'

'Any reason other than jealousy?'

'Jane jealous?' It was a new idea to me. 'She has her own life. She sees me perhaps three times a year. Until now there's been nothing but business between us.' I stared at the oak beams in the ceiling.

'Until now.'

I decided to take a vacation from this line of talk. 'Did

you know,' I began at once, 'that when you sleep your face loses every sign of ... um, there's a sort of grace note of pain if you don't smile. But it's not there when you're asleep.'

'I probably regress in sleep to my life before I met Moey.' She smiled lopsidedly. 'Since then, there's been a – what did you call it? – grace note of pain.'

'He didn't look that hard to take. Universal grandpa.'

Her breasts swung as she suddenly sat up, arm angled, head propped in her hand. Her sable-dark eyes surveyed me with a sort of clinical detachment. 'He has other girls, you know.'

I said nothing.

'That scenario you laid on me last night. The meeting at a cast party, the beach house in Malibu. Mostly on target, but it all happened a lot earlier in my life. It happened the third month I was in New York. It was 1960.' She took a long breath. 'I was sixteen.'

'Jailbait.' I gave her a stern look. 'That dirty old man. It makes you, um ...'

'Save your grey cells. I'm thirty-three.'

'Had you pegged five years younger.'

'This is the morning after. You don't have to be a gentleman any more.'

We lay that way for a long while, watching each other. 'The statute of limitations ran out some time ago,' I observed.

'On what?'

'Oh, contributing to the delinquency of a minor.'

She grinned with a sort of perverse delight. 'You see what it is, then. When I sleep, I'm back at age fifteen or earlier. Before the *gevainte punim*.'

'The what?'

'It's a Yiddish phrase my agent warned me about. "Smile a lot, bubby," he keeps telling me, "because you gotta real *gevainte punim*." A face full of pain. One of the reasons I haven't had all that many big parts in flicks.'

I nodded. 'It would go well, though, with the role of Ursula in *Licence to Kill*. She's a lady with troubles.'

Her mind clicked into another channel suddenly. 'You don't want me at your editor's party tonight.'

'It'll do wonders for my image.'

'Not for mine with Moey. Alone in your room is one thing. At a publishing party is another. They gossip a lot, publishing people.'

'Who says actresses aren't practical?' I asked rhetorically, getting out of bed and heading for the shower. 'We'll leave separately now and meet down the street for elevenses at the Ritz. Being Yanks, we'll call it brunch.'

'You're on.'

I left the apartment ahead of her and found a pleasant table, streaked with warm sun. So far my London stay had been marked by particularly good weather. And God knew my love life had never before been quite so full. I nursed a Bloody Mary until noon and then decided I'd been stood up.

Going to the porter's box at the Arlington Street side of the Ritz, I placed a call to Blue's Hotel and asked for Rosalind's suite. No one answered the ring and the operator volunteered the information that he hadn't seen her since yesterday. I seemed to do well enough in the night, but women did have a tendency towards walking out on me in the morning.

But it was still, after all, a delightful day. I strolled along Piccadilly and at White Horse Street turned into the long, narrow lane towards Shepherd Market.

Jane Tait's wine-and-cheese place looked deserted. I moved out of the Market towards Grosvenor Square again and stood at the foot of it, staring across at the three buildings that I'd forgotten all night to do any thinking about. My publisher's looked closed, the Manhattan Bank and Trust Company even more so. But the Marine guard in front of the US Embassy was a sign of life on a lazy Saturday.

I have good hunches. We all do. I've been trained to

act on them. It had been a hunch that had made me lock on to Jean-Luc Dorani at La Place that night. All the rest followed, and eventually, put me in the lounge when Dorani and Moe Gordon had met. And when Dave Greeley had his private audience with Moey-baby.

Hunches have put me where I am today, wherever that is. It isn't always easy to trust them, but if one doesn't label them hunches, but call them something like, um, extrasensory messages, then they're easy to follow.

I had been struck by the hunch that if I could get into my cubbyhole and listen to my little FM bug, it would, as Personal ads put it, 'be to my advantage'. This was the telegram ESP had just delivered.

I managed to find a porter at my publisher's who, fortunately, remembered that I had a temporary office assigned to me. He insisted on escorting me all the way to my cubbyhole. There was a slight look of betrayal on his face when I closed the door and locked it from the inside.

I switched on the set and immediately heard a low, crackling static sound. But FM is static-free. Nor was this the ordinary static or background noise. It had a pulsating quality to it. Then it stopped. There were clinking sounds. The hum began again.

Clearly, I was listening to activity inside the bank vault. Illegal activity, but industrious activity nevertheless.

So much for Dave Greeley's super-sensitive electronic noise detector and alarm. The bank had wasted three thousand pounds sterling on it. The noise was there, but no alarm.

Unless, of course, there was a way of shorting out the alarm. At the close of yesterday's business, when the vault door was swung shut and the time-release box activated for nine-thirty Monday, someone had made sure the super-sensitive alarm wouldn't work.

There were several ways to do that. A properly trained man who returned after a late lunch Friday in the persona of Dave Greeley would have time to choose a method of shorting out the mechanism.

And, all weekend, someone could raise bloody noisy hell in that vault without triggering any alarm.

I left my cubbyhole, slipped the porter a pound note and went in search of something that probably didn't exist. What I wanted was a very large-scale map of London in which each square, each block was clearly defined, as if for an architect, in such a way that one could make an educated guess as to how long it would take, using a battery-operated electric drill, to get through the vast wall of limestone that separated the basement of the United States Embassy from the inner vault, around the corner, of the Manhattan Bank and Trust Company, Mayfair branch.

CHAPTER TWELVE

I checked a few places in the tourist area of Mayfair and the shops towards Piccadilly and Oxford Road, then hailed a cab for Beauchamp Place not far from Harrods, where there was a marvellous map store. No luck there, either, and now it was one o'clock.

I had no accurate idea of how hi-fi my little Uher bug was as a listening instrument, but it seemed to me that the drilling sounds it was picking up were still quite muted, perhaps by several feet of limestone.

To add to the general climate of ignorance, I had no accurate idea what sort of security routine was kept at the US Embassy. After all, this wasn't Moscow; one might imagine the precautions as being minimal, but there had to be a few, nevertheless.

Which led to the thought that the determined drillers were not about to blast their way into the vault with any form of explosive, neither on a Saturday nor a Sunday. Embassies have no days off. There would always be some staff on hand to hear the explosion, even if no automatic sensor device picked it up. So it was drill, drill, drill.

If all this hazy thinking were halfway reliable, I mused, walking back from Knightsbridge through Green Park to my hotel, then the drillers would have a long, slow time of it. For all I knew, they planned on making the break-in a life's career, a little drilling now, some more later. After all, with the fake Dave Greeley on duty and in charge of the alarm system, they had a true licence to steal.

The ersatz Greeley had been an inspiration on the part of the planners. It isn't easy, in case you've entertained thoughts of replacing someone with a physical double. It requires two things: a widespread organization and tremendous clout.

Money isn't enough. One has to have the network of agents who can locate such a double. Then one needs the power of life and death to keep the new man's mouth shut tight, now and forever.

There aren't that many organizations that fill both criteria. I imagine MI5 might, or another nation's spy apparatus, even our own feckless CIA. Or the organization to which both Moe Gordon and Jean-Luc Dorani had top-level access.

The fate of the imitation Greeley was no concern of mine. To be truthful, I didn't much care what they'd done with the original model, but it came to me that if I laid my plans carefully, the missing Dave might give me a reason to muck about inside the US Embassy. To do that, I would need some things I had in my room at the hotel, which was why I was returning there.

I suppose it was the fine weather that tempted me to walk back. In any event, I got a break I badly needed. If I'd taken a cab I might never have discovered that I'd, as the technical phrase puts it, picked up a tail.

I'd left Green Park and was moving along with the holiday crowd on Piccadilly as they paused to view the truly bad works of art hung on the park fence. This kind of art seems to crop up wherever an outdoor exhibition area is available. There were the usual drawings of forlorn children with immense eyes, clowns in tears, jolly tramps with cigar-butts, lush nudes painted on black velvet and the ever-present vintage autos constructed of bits of clock parts. Did I forget the spatter paintings, or the statuettes of welded horseshoe nails? Unlike the nearly identical displays in, say, Rome's Piazza Navona or Manhattan's Greenwich Village, this collection did manage to include a few clinically pornographic oils – are gynaecologists painting these days? – and some not-bad architectural renderings of London buildings.

I had paused before one of the latter. Out of the corner of my eye I saw him stop short too quickly for a typical stroller. He was trying to keep his distance from me as I strode past this assortment of non-art. My fast stop had caught him by surprise.

I turned stroller now, starting, stopping unpredictably. He matched my pattern precisely. In such a situation it's no good trying to spot your follower's face. He'll understand you've spotted him and that will be that. But I had to know what he looked like.

At the Green Park underground station I crossed Piccadilly, as if heading into Mayfair, then ducked downstairs. I waited a count of five, hoping he'd dash down the stairs on his side of Piccadilly, hoping to catch me below decks. When I ran back topside, he'd disappeared.

I zigzagged back across Piccadilly traffic to the park side and lurked behind some shrubbery. It was with a certain sense of gratification that I watched him emerge at street level a while later, looking miffed as he stared about him for a while.

He was hardly thirty, dressed in a very good visitor-to-London-from-perhaps-the-Continent costume, the Italian flared slacks, clingingly skimpy French shirt, ubiquitous red sweater folded across his backside with the arms tied in front. He could have been any young European except that he had US written all over his face and curly blond hair.

After a while he hailed a cab and left. I moved out of hiding and continued through the park, staying in the open to spot anyone Curly might have had helping him. There was no one, however. As an object of surveillance, I was a low-budget item.

I sat down on a bench and considered life. Had he been with me all morning? I'm an old hand, but us grizzled greybeards don't always spot a tail that fast. Some are too adept to be spotted, a category in which I didn't quite include Curly.

Had he followed me from Blue's? What had he made

of my stopover at my publisher's? More to the point, who was paying him? Uncle?

No trick to Uncle's knowing where I was. It would be elementary police work, made all the easier since Uncle and John Bull cooperate fully at the nitty-gritty level of who's-sleeping-where-in-London. If Curly had picked me up at Blue's, had he also made Moe Gordon? Or Roz?

What about my earlier trip to the electronics supply shop on Beak Street? Had he spotted Jack Philemon? My visits to Dave Greeley's bank?

I gritted my teeth at my own carelessness. I'd been so cool when it came to Gordon and Dorani. But why had I been dumb enough to forget that Uncle still kept an interest in my comings and goings?

The anxiety fit passed after a while. I was giving Uncle too much credit and not enough to me. If I'd spotted Curly today, wouldn't I have spotted him before today? He wasn't that good. I was pretty good. I had to work on the assumption that the surveillance had not begun until today.

Then the mood of doubt closed in again. Had I spotted him too easily? There were only two possible answers. Well, more than two, actually. An infinite number of which two seemed likeliest.

One. Curly was not Uncle's. He was merely a button-man on someone else's payroll. Gordon's perhaps.

Two – and this one gave me gooseflesh – I had been meant to spot him.

Meant to! If so, had the slim youngster with the curly hair been sent as a warning? Of what? By whom?

CHAPTER THIRTEEN

There is a point in these affairs when one still retains the right to bow out of 'it'. This was such a moment.

Till now all I'd known for certain was that I'd found my way into something lucrative. But the only way I work well is when no one is watching my moves. That freedom was now at an end.

So far I'd kept myself disconnected from 'it'. Although I planned to use Jack Philemon later on, I'd even kept him out of things. I was operating at least one remove from the centre of 'it', which accounted for my ignorance of what it really was.

But now I knew something else. I was being watched. The odds against my successfully getting into 'it' had now shifted unfavourably. If I were as prudent as I liked to think I was, now was the time to bail out.

Perhaps, if Curly's appearance actually was a warning, the message of the warning was just that: keep out of 'it'.

I got up from the park bench and walked slowly towards Blue's. I'd put quite a bit of time and effort into this project, whatever the hell it was. At each step of the way, my original intuition had been proved right. The hunch that had carried me here had been a good one. Should I protect my investment to the extent of seeing what the next development would be? Or should I get smart and bow out?

So thinking, and without deciding a damned thing, I turned the corner into St James's and walked along the driveway into Blue's.

'Beg pardon, Mr Patrick, sir,' the desk man said in an

undertone. 'We're making our apologies to guests today. Something's happened to our cleaning ladies. Both of them are late and you'll find your room unmade. We've got temps laid on and ought to have the situation in hand within the hour.'

I nodded and went upstairs, opened the door to my room and had already closed it behind me before I realized that the desk man was a master of understatement.

The place was a wreck. Rosalind and I had done a few energetic things in places other than the bed during the previous evening, but none of them accounted for the scene I was now viewing.

There had obviously been one hell of a fight here after I'd left this morning. The sheets and pillows were off the bed. One sheet, in fact, had been ripped across. A chair was overturned and someone had knocked all the glasses off the bar near the refrigerator.

I went to the telephone and was about to pick it up when I thought better of the idea. Something had begun to emit warning clicks at the back of my head, as if a Geiger counter had been implanted there. No maids today? My room trashed? What about Roz's suite?

Blue's isn't that big a hotel. I think there are four floors and perhaps thirty rooms. I didn't know the number of her suite but she'd mentioned that we were on the same floor – Fortuna omnia vincit – and that she had a view into the courtyard. It wasn't too hard to find what had to be her door. I knocked and got no answer.

In the door-rattling profession – the burglar gents who prowl hotel corridors shaking doors to find who's in and who's out – the only weapon a self-respecting thief carries is called a 'loid'. This is a stiff bit of celluloid (any credit card will do), by means of which, with some tricky sideways pressure on the doorknob, one can tease back the catch of quite a few more hotel doors than the management would like to admit.

I loided my way into Roz's suite. Of Rosalind Rue there

wasn't a sign. I found none of her clothes or cosmetics. Nothing marked her seemingly hasty and enforced departure. Unless one counted the large steamer trunk in the middle of the living room.

I looked it over. When was the last time you or anyone you know travelled with a steamer trunk? Most cabbies won't touch one. Neither will airlines. The steamer trunk symbolizes a way of travelling that hasn't really existed for several decades now.

And, while I know that actresses frequently travel with extensive wardrobes, a steamer trunk is not how they transport things. No Red Cap, Sky Cap or porter is equipped to handle anything that large and, in most of the railroad stations of the world, there aren't any porters anyway.

I shoved the trunk. It wasn't terribly heavy, but it did seem to have something in it. There is no way to loid a trunk. The preferred instrument is a beer-can opener. It pops the recessed latches wide open with the twist of a wrist. The little bar had something in the corkscrew line and after a few minutes the locks gave. I swung the two halves of the trunk open.

She was naked, tied with strips of torn sheet, probably looted from my bed. The idea was total restraint without telltale marks. A gag of bed linen muffled her lovely mouth. All her clothes had been stuffed in around her, as if cushioning a fragile load for shipment. Her eyes were closed and she was breathing shallowly.

No one likes to admit to as much intimate knowledge of crime as I have. But the fact remains that for us literary experts crimes have trademarks. The artificial embolism, for example, injected into a hospital patient, is known in the trade as the Sicilian Air Bubble, so often do the minions of organized crime use the method. The long icepick introduced into the brain via the ear, to conceal for a while its entry wound, bears the trademark of the Magaddino mob and is known as the Buffalo Hat Pin. And if there is one patented method by which the European gangs handle the enforced travel of someone not yet slated for death, the steamer trunk is it.

I lifted her out. Underneath her was a kind of large, leatherbound scrapbook, with a lock, as on a diary. Whoever had stripped and stashed her here would return as soon as he'd organized a pickup truck. She felt weightless as I carried her and her scrapbook back to my room and locked us in.

I removed the gag and bonds, but nothing about her changed; breathing still shallow, obviously the result of some extremely powerful sedative injection. In drugged repose, she had lost the hurt look. So much for what appearances tell us – namely, nothing.

If the gentleman entrusted with her disposal came back now and found her gone, they would be careless indeed if they didn't check my room first. After all they'd found her here. I reached the conclusion that she and I were both in trouble.

To get Rosalind Rue out of the hotel I had exactly the same problem as her original abductors. At any moment they would be arriving with whatever transport they planned to use, probably an almost anonymous van. This was precisely the vehicle I would need, since there is no real chance of carrying an unconscious woman out of a hotel and into a passing taxi. Not these days.

I didn't know Blue's Hotel that well. It might, for example, have been a wholly owned subsidiary of organized crime, but I didn't think so. When the mob goes into the hotel business – as it does regularly – there are certain tell-tale signs. The furnishings, for example, are usually redone a touch more garish. I believe the phrase is 'livening up things a little' – usually with touches of Etruscan red, moss green and lotsa gilt.

Then the concessions in the hotel become very expense-accounty. Certain international jewellers and furriers set up shop. Gambling arrives if there is the remote chance of installing it legally.

So does a theatre ticket office, higher prices on the bar

drinks and usually, to cap the changeover, one public room becomes a nightclub or disco where the usual tired show-biz celebs who trot the Mafia entertainment circuit from Las Vegas to the Bahamas to Cannes like so many mechanical ducks in a shooting gallery begin to make regular appearances. So do their friends, in the audience. Every week is Old Home Week because the Gang's All Here.

Blue's had none of those stigmata. My chances of getting Roz out of the hotel were thus, at least, even-odds. But how?

I checked her condition as well as I could, not having an MD after my name. My early conclusion, that she was out like a light for hours to come, seemed reconfirmed. No help from that quarter. Black coffee, forcing her to walk back and forth, all those tried truisms of private-eye films, wouldn't help. Come to think of it, the one private eye I knew in London, Jack Philemon, might have come in handy about now. But, apart from lending a hand physically, what else could Jack have done? And the nasties who were exporting Roz's lovely nude body would be returning at any moment.

My best way out was to hi-jack their abduction. Would they bring the van to the front of Blue's? Not likely. There had to be a service entrance through which steamer trunks and other arcane memorabilia got loaded and unloaded.

I swung my ravaged bed to one side, laid my sable-haired naked lady and her diary gently on the floor, and carefully rolled the bed back over her. It wasn't much as camouflage, but it might work if she didn't snore.

Downstairs, I strolled past the desk with a nod and a smile and walked out into the courtyard where cabs made their U-turn to pick up and deliver guests. No doorman at the moment. I slipped sideways around the back of Blue's. There was, in fact, a sort of one-horse loading area into which, at that precise moment, a very harassed fellow was backing a small dark-blue Escort van.

He wasn't familiar with the vehicle – having probably just stolen it – and was concentrating closely on manoeuvring. That was why he didn't see me. I assumed his confrère would already be on his way upstairs to get the steamer trunk in motion.

He braked the van and switched off the engine, then hopped out and started to disappear around the back of the van towards the loading platform.

I dodged the other way around, jumping up on the concrete ramp. That was why, when we collided at the rear of the truck, I was a foot above him and prepared.

I am terrible with my fists. One ought to state that early in the game. I am much better with lengths of heavy iron, pokers, golf clubs, anything but fists. The kind of work I do doesn't toughen fingers and knuckles. In a real boxing fray, I would cripple myself with the first few punches.

I butted him in the face with the top of my head.

This is a very hard weapon, indeed, and an unsuspected one. There is a point to one side of the chin where the trigeminal nerve passes close enough so that a blow to it can induce unconsciousness. I missed it.

The blow stunned him, however, and he dropped to his knees. I brought my own right knee up and managed to find the correct spot on the chin this time. His eyes – big ripe olives – rolled up in his head and he pitched sideways on to the tiny brick pavement.

I opened the back of the van and was pleased to see that his partner wasn't there. I dragged my sleeping boy into the van and closed the door on us. With my luck he might come awake at any moment, but something about the way his head had hit the bricks made me think I had more time than that.

I rummaged around in the van's tool kit until I found that all-purpose length of rod which serves as a jack-handle and a spanner for the lug nuts that hold the wheel to the brake drum. I felt a lot better now, although the top of my head was throbbing.

87

We waited in ambush, the sleeper and I. Five minutes went by. I assumed the missing confederate had already discovered the empty trunk. He might even have checked my room and possibly other places as well, including the desk clerk who would, of course, have nothing to tell him about a wandering naked brunette. I hoped the man wasn't in the habit of looking under beds.

Another chunk of five minutes passed in what seemed hours. I decided that we could none of us wait much longer. Leaving the sleeping man, I made my way on to the loading platform and inside the hotel.

No one rushed me. No one shouted or pointed a finger. It began to dawn on me that there was no other man. There never had been. That was why my room had been wrecked. One man pitted against one woman would have accounted for the ferocity of the struggle. Two men could have pulled the snatch without demolishing the premises.

It wasn't like Moe to send only one man. Had he run out of flunkies, or were the rest elsewhere employed on even more nefarious work? If he'd hoped to snatch Rozzie on the cheap, it had been a dubious economy.

I found a luggage elevator also used by room service and the missing clean-up brigade. In the laundry room I located one of those white canvas hand-carts in which linen is wheeled about. I took it up the service elevator to the top floor and rolled it into my room .

Pulling aside the bed, I lifted Roz and her leather-bound scrapbook into the laundry hamper on wheels. I have mentioned, I believe, that she was not a big woman, except in some key places? All of them showed to added advantage in her present state of undress. The hamper was a small one and badly designed for the purpose to which I wanted to put it. Jane Tait, for instance, who was five-ten in heels, would never have fitted in it. Roz did, with a sheet over her to ward off pneumonia.

Smiling slightly at the fantasy of bundling my editor naked into a laundry basket, surely something every writer has dreamed of, I wheeled Roz to the service lift and down we went. Getting her in the van was easy, now that she'd been equipped with wheels.

Slowly the van moved out of the service area of Blue's, circled the courtyard and out into St James's. I steered left into the one-way traffic that headed uphill towards Piccadilly. Another left and I was driving along Piccadilly itself, past the same sad line-up of artists' paintings I'd inspected just an hour before. In the back of the van, my olive-eyed sleeper grunted something unintelligible, but he remained asleep.

I drove past the same Green Park underground where I'd shaken off Curly. Had I really hoped, as recently as an hour ago, that I still had the option of getting out of 'it'?

Or was I now being taught that I'd committed the supreme beginner's mistake in this sort of business, the capital error of thinking I knew the cast of characters. This was a game of masks, of reverses, of façades, all dimly perceived behind a scrim.

What did I know? That something very big had brought Jean-Luc Dorani to the States under a cloak of official protection so solid that it passed him in and out of the country without a hitch.

What else did I know? That Dorani's first act on arrival had been to huddle with Moe Gordon. I also knew that, while Dorani could crisscross US Immigration effortlessly, of late Moe Gordon had exiled himself from the US. Was he wanted back home?

Anything beyond that? Well, the switch of Dave Greeley at the bank, an embarrassing bit of information. I knew it but I didn't know what it meant. Just as I knew someone was tunnelling into the vault but didn't know what he was looking for.

Beyond these known things, all was smoke and scrim. I glanced in the rear-view mirror of the van and saw an exceedingly grim look on my face. Why had I elected to become the protector of an actress clad only in a skinful of enough soporifics to stun a horse? Why had I elected to stay in 'it' against all common sense?

CHAPTER FOURTEEN

Will you agree with the proposition that leading a regular life is important? Who can argue the point? The lady in the hamper, for example, was living proof that a life of shifts and changes, of comings and goings was not only unstable but led to being stripped to the buff, injected with soporifics and trundled through the streets of London like wet wash.

On the other hand, Jane Tait had always led the most regular life of anyone I knew. Five years before, when her parents had emigrated to Australia, she had elected to remain in London and take over their rather extensive flat in that part of Kensington called Campden Hill Road, near the Duchess of Bedford's Walk.

I had been there a dozen times since, I suppose, always giving the address to a cabbie and letting him worry. Now that I was the driver, and of a vehicle whose gears and clutch were unfamiliar to me, I managed to get myself thoroughly lost. It was no good asking a policeman. If I knew anything about the blue van, I knew it had been custom-stolen for the occasion and might well be out on report by now.

Somewhere off Old Brompton Road I came to a cemetery, where I laid my olive-eyed boy to rest amid well-cropped grass. All of this, plus mistakes in driving, took quite a bit of time.

Thus it was that I finally reached the Tait place as the early dusk of April was closing down over London. The growing darkness was my only bright spot, if I may use the paradox. I'll spare you the irate dialogue from Jane.

With a party to prepare for, she was being asked to come downstairs and help me get a laundry hamper into her flat.

We managed to fit it into the arthritic elevator and take it up to her floor, wheel it inside her flat and straight to a maid's bedroom in the rear of the place that I remembered from my last visit.

'Max,' Jane Tait said through clenched teeth, 'will you now tell me what this is all about?'

'Lift the sheet off the hamper.'

She did so, instantly, with a twitch like the crack of a whip. Then she stood for a long time gazing down at Sleeping Beauty. Slowly, Jane's lovely, long face lifted and, slowly, it turned towards me.

'Max,' she asked. 'What ... is ... the meaning ... of this?'

'I told you I was bringing a girl.'

She barely suppressed a gasp of rage. 'Did she take too many downers, or what?'

'There was a kidnap I stumbled into almost by accident.'

'People will be here in a couple of hours,' she said in a very flat unstressed tone, as if speaking to someone she hardly knew and wanted to keep as a stranger. 'We'll have to hide her in here, I suppose.'

'This is really very good of you.'

'What other choice do you offer? Who kidnapped her?'

'Don't know.'

'What happens when my guests start to arrive?'

I smiled uneasily. 'I have no idea when she'll come to.'

We heaved Roz, naked, on to the small bed. Jane Tait sighed in exasperation. 'I suppose,' she said then, 'if that's the type one likes, it's a good example of the type.'

'Don't you have a robe for her?'

She made a noise with her mouth analogous to the snapping of a pencil, turned and left the room. She came back with a flowered wrapper, into which we managed to wrestle Roz. I had the idea it was the oldest robe avail-

able. Then we tucked her under the sheets. 'Extra blanket,
I should think,' Jane Tait said aloud, but to herself.

She picked up the large, leather-bound scrapbook. 'Is
this hers?' I nodded. 'The lock's smashed,' she observed.

'I know.'

'Have you looked inside?'

'Not I.'

'Not much.'

She spread a second blanket over the sleeping woman,
then turned to me with a certain fastidious reluctance.
'Max, two conditions.'

'Ten if you wish.'

'Just two. I will not have her coming out of it in the
middle of the party and wandering among the guests like
Banquo's ghost. That's your responsibility. Do you understand?'

'Perfectly.'

'The second condition is that when this is over you *will*
explain it. You will *not* weasel out. Is that clear?'

'Small enough price to pay for your help.'

Her grey-blue eyes narrowed. She folded her long arms
over her breasts and watched me for a moment. 'I am not
as innocent as you imagine, Max. I have the distinct feeling that, before this is over, you'll need even more help.
Tell me something.'

'Anything, dear heart.'

Her mouth turned a bit malicious. 'Do you know what
the hell you're doing?'

'Until I found her trussed up in a steamer trunk? Yes.'

Her eyes shot wide open. 'That's awful. Who cou —?'

'Part of the full explanation.'

'I mean it, Max. You can't slough me off any more. I
don't want to have to wait two years and read about this
in one of your thinly disguised novels of the absurd.'

'You'll be the first to know. The only, if I can help it.'

The strained look left her and she turned human again.
'That's better, then.' She found a piece of paper and a
pencil. 'Write her a note. Tell her she's fine and not to

try pounding on the door. Because we have to lock her in now.'

'Yes, good idea.'

'My God,' she exclaimed then. 'Just think if I still had my old bachelor flat. You'd have had to cruise the streets with her till the party was over.' She cellophane-taped my note to the inside of the door and we left Roz to herself. Jane Tait turned the key and handed it to me. 'Remember now.'

'Word of honour.'

We turned to see the laundry hamper. 'I'll, um, run that back downstairs now and take it away in the van,' I promised. 'Be back after I park the thing somewhere far away.'

'High Street Ken,' she suggested. 'Near Barker's? Lots of traffic there. Easy to overlook a parked van.'

'I don't care if the cops find it,' I said. 'I just don't want it found downstairs. See you.'

When I got back half an hour later, I unlocked Roz's prison cell and checked her over. Either they had given her some awfully strong stuff, or a lot of it. I began to wonder if she needed a doctor, but her colour seemed fine and her breathing regular. I felt her pulse, which told me nothing except that her heart had not ceased to beat and was, in fact, thudding along at a fairly steady rate. I locked her in and went to Jane Tait in the kitchen.

'I'm not dressed for a party,' I said.

She surveyed me as I stood there in tan Levis and a blue denim wrangler's jacket over a black turtleneck shirt. 'You'll do fine.'

'Can I help with anything? We have an hour.'

She stood watching me, as if not believing what she saw. 'Max, this domestic streak in you is very unsettling. Just stay the same lying son of a bitch I've always known and loved, will you?'

'No radish rosettes to carve?'

'Would you like to take a celery stalk and stuff it?'

CHAPTER FIFTEEN

You should have been there. No, really, Jane Tait's parties are always good, but this one was, as one woman kept telling me all evening, 's-you-pah!' I agreed with her, but I had my own reasons. What made the party super was that I had a place to which I could retreat from time to time.

At some parties one can stroll out in the garden, or have a smoke on the balcony. Here I had a maid's room far from the madding crowd to which I reported about every twenty minutes as if I'd been on sentry duty. The peaceful slumber in which Roz lay made me resolve to find out just what sort of stiff they'd pumped into her. It was fantastic. I wanted some for myself.

Meanwhile, back at the party, everyone had introduced me not once but several times to the only other novelist, a self-important little fellow about my age whose latest work had made the English best-seller lists. Ian Goodman, our mutual publisher, told us both that we had a lot in common.

'Does one?' the novelist asked the first time Ian said this.

'One doesn't, actually,' he said on the second introduction half an hour later.

Jane Tait's secret of party-giving was simply to delay the food until we were all smashed. This Plimsoll mark was reached at about nine p.m. and from then on my recollection, although steady, became a bit flawed.

There was, for example, Ian's girlfriend, a short, dark, pretty girl with a Welsh name like Bronwen or some-

95

thing, who kept stroking him and pecking his cheek with her pouty lips. At one point, as I made her a fresh drink, she managed to loosen her gaze from Ian, across the room, and stare for a moment into my face.

'You're Max Patrick,' she disclosed.

'Where did you hear that?'

Bronwen frowned. 'Well, but you're an American. You don't deny that.'

'Caught.'

She took her drink from me. 'I'm Welsh. Real troglodyte stock. Scooped out skull and all.' She took my free hand and placed it on top of her head. There was a flatness there, almost a concavity.

'Is that, um, Welsh?'

'Pre-Celt. The Old People.' Her glance wavered and swung about the room till it located Ian. 'We have to be up early tomorrow. You will help me.'

'Tomorrow's Sunday. Who's we? And what the hell can I do to help?'

'In which order?' she asked crossly. 'Never mind. We is Ian. We leave early to drive up Stratford way for a big Shakespearean luncheon. But he'll want to gamble when we leave here tonight. You have to keep him out of the casinos.'

'How?'

'Come with us. He'll behave if you're there. Make sure we get back to our flat by midnight.' She walked across the room without another word.

I had always understood that Ian was married and had children. At least, on his desk stood a picture of three small girls. But perhaps he'd split with his wife to set up housekeeping with a genuine troglodyte.

A slim, older man with grey elf-locks and a black Nikon with f/1.4 lens had been circulating all evening, snapping pictures by available light. I gathered he had Jane Tait's permission. He appeared at the bar now. 'Just keep on making that drink, love,' he murmured, focusing on me. The Nikon's shutter did its velvety whispering click.

'You're not here on some sort of assignment?'

'Lord, no.' He snapped a second shot. 'Not for the press, that is. I've been doing this at London parties for a year now. Simply miles of negs. There has to be a book in it, don't you think?'

I thought. 'Well,' I said then, 'if there's a book in going around taping what people say and transcribing it on paper, then I guess there's a book in what you're doing.'

'Don't be anal, love.'

He blew me a kiss and moved on. In five minutes I was due for another check of the maid's room. Everyone was standing about in clumps between me and the escape doorway, which was why, without wanting to, I squished into a two-point collision with a big, plump, hearty lady with breasts like bumper guards and a face like a pug dog.

'Whell,' she said in an explosive way, 'at least you know they're not falsies.'

'Christ, lady, my grandmother told me about falsies. How old are you?'

It wasn't the most tactful question in my repertoire. She drew herself up until we were precisely eyeball-to-eyeball. 'And to think that I adored *Licence to Kill*,' she responded. 'I tried to get you on my show but you were in Tasmania or somewhere. Is it true Fortune's taken an option on it for the movies?'

'It wasn't Tasmania. It was Antofagasta, where the guano comes from.'

I moved out of the room, but not too quickly to hear her tell someone: 'Not at all what one would expect from the novels.'

When I looked in on Roz she had shifted position slightly and was on her side. I took this to mean she might be coming out of the stuff any hour now. Back at the party, Jane Tait pulled me over to one side of the big playpen.

'What did you do to Maggie Whelk?'

'Which is Maggie Whelk.'

She indicated Brunnhilde of the Bosoms.

'Did I insult her?'

'She wants you to do her six o'clock show next week.'

'She's in television?'

My editor gave me a pained frown. 'How is the invisible guest?'

'Safe and sound. You see that dark, little girl?'

'Bronwen?'

'I thought Ian was married.'

'Separated. You don't remember Bronwen, then? She had the office next to mine. We were both senior editors.'

'Were?'

'She's the editor in chief now.'

The English do things much more directly than the Americans, after all. Bedfellows make strange office politics. 'Max, here's our other captive novelist of the evening. Have you two met?'

'Endlessly,' the other writer told her.

'You must have a lot to talk about.'

'No, we don't,' I assured her, and walked away.

I try not to associate with writers – a dull lot, either silently saving their gems for print or babbling endlessly at the centre of attention. Occasionally, of course, another writer and I will find something of mutual interest to discuss at a party, but it's never the technical tricks of the trade. I mean, there are no secrets. Plain white bond paper, double-space the typing on one side of the page and leave a good left-hand margin. What else is there to know?

But when we do get to talking, it centres on the universal topic of how to hold on to what money we earn. Tax dodges, havens, Swiss accounts, Luxembourg corporations, estates in Ireland, Grand Cayman trusts, residence in the Channel Islands ... that's what writers talk about. Is it better, for example, to marry a Canadian woman and deed your royalties to her because of the new wrinkle in Canadian tax law? Are there any attractive Canadian women? What about the tax moratorium for immigrants to Malta? But Malta is just a pink limestone old folks' home. Have they got the IRS to treat royalties like earned income? Rotten bastards.

I have often wondered why. If I were to run into a personal favourite, say Lawrence Durrell, why could we not discuss, um, *big* topics like, um, dramatizing the universal condition of man? Instead of tax-free Bahamian certificates of deposit.

Most of the group had now flocked to the buffet where Jane Tait's dinner had finally materialized. I decided writing was a chancy business. If one took sick, no one else finished one's novel or paid the doctor bills. Being freelances, we had no fringe benefits, no retirement pensions, severance pay. We weren't even eligible for employment compensation in the States. The comfy certainties of modern jobs, the welfare provisions of governments and trade unions were not for us. So we worried, incessantly, about money. In the lives of Balzac or Dostoyevsky, one notes that this obsession is by no means a new thing among writers.

Which is why, not to be too coy about it, I had some years ago branched out into a sideline business. Which Jane Tait had stumbled on to, I knew.

The lighter-than-air photographer was busily shooting cruel studies of people eating. Have you ever noticed we're at our worst biting into something? The animal shows.

A tall young man in a blazer, open shirt and foulard knotted around his bare throat came over with two plates of food and handed one to me. 'You look stuck on dead centre,' he observed.

John had been my editor when I'd been with another publisher. His firm had lost me to Jane Tait's company, but John and I had stayed friends. 'Thanks,' I said, taking the plate.

'The new book's doing well. And they've got a pile for paperback rights, I hear.' He took a bit of smoked salmon. 'We were outbid by a mile.'

'Not your fault, I'm sure.'

'There ought to be a way we can win you back. These people are getting away with murder on your contract.'

I grinned at him. 'They're still paying more than your outfit.'

'Maybe I can do something about that.'

'Finish the sentence.'

'There's some thought I may move to another house.'

I laughed at him. If it wasn't writers hopping from publisher to publisher, it was editors who played musical chairs. 'When you land somewhere, let me know.'

'I may work for Ian. Will that make a problem for you with Jane?'

'In what way?'

'I had heard ... you two ...' He let it die away again.

I ate in silence for a moment. The grapevine in London worked even more quickly than in New York. About all it would have to work on was a lunch or two, unless someone had seen Jane Tait leaving Blue's Hotel one morning and put two and two together. Or had she told a girlfriend? Didn't seem her style.

'You're daft,' I told him.

By eleven o'clock we had all settled down to doing or watching the trademarked numbers all of us did at parties. The big woman, Maggie Whelk, usurped stage centre for a tearful personal memoire of having learned, when in her twenties, that she had a half-sister she never knew existed, of searching for her, of tracking her down and finding—

'That you had nothing at all in common,' someone ended the story for her. Evidently they'd all heard it before.

'Is that all there is?' someone else sang raucously.

'Except that the half-sister was a Soho scrubber who did rubber mac tricks for five bob a flog,' someone else bawled out.

'That was before she ran for Parliament,' another voice added. I had the feeling no one would mind if I skipped the party for a few moments, least of all me. I slipped back to the maid's room. Roz had shifted position again, one hand under the pillow. I sat down on the edge of the bed and shook her gently by the shoulders. She muttered something, but remained asleep. I shook her again. This time she failed to respond.

Her scrapbook, or whatever it was, had been left on the bedside table. I opened it and saw that it was, in fact, only a scrapbook of clippings and snapshots, although here and there she had written a few paragraphs.

The book didn't seem to be organized chronologically. It began more or less in the middle of things with a newspaper clipping, a photograph of Roz on skis executing a rather tight turn, knees flexed, poles working. The caption didn't accompany the photo, but she had penned in the legend 'Aspen, 1970'.

I leafed quickly through the scrapbook and saw entries from as far back as 1960. I closed the book without really studying it, and tried shaking her awake again. She remained motionless and asleep.

I got up and pitched the book at the table. It fell open, to the floor. I saw, on a page by itself, a mounted eight-by-ten-inch glossy photograph of John F. Kennedy. Someone had written on the scrapbook page, not on the photo, the line from an Irving Berlin song:

'I'll be loving you ... always.'

A queer chill shot across my shoulder blades. I closed the book so quickly it made the sound of a shot. The quotation had been in a different hand from the other captions in the book.

I sat there silently for the longest time, remembering, thinking. Elsewhere in the apartment the party was getting louder as it drew to a close. There would be a core of die-hards, however, who would be here till early Sunday morning. I didn't want to be here with them, nor did I want Roz here. But there was really nowhere else for me to take her until she was able to walk under her own power.

I stared at the closed scrapbook with its mutilated lock.

A schoolgirl idea, locking the book. A schoolgirl crush on a handsome president? There had been other women in Kennedy's life, some of them actresses.

I sat there, wondering how many of the others had also been the personal protégé of Moe Gordon.

Caption of a photograph from the San Diego *Times-Union*, 27 July:

Among the avid fans of golfing in the gallery that watched the fourth annual open invitation tournament at Rancho La Costa last week were, left to right: singer Paul Sedotti, film director Budd West, investment counsellor Moe Gordon, Senator John F. Kennedy and starlet Rosalind Rue.

CHAPTER SIXTEEN

The last guest was ushered out around two in the morning. I watched Jane go into the kitchen. There didn't seem to be anything we wanted to say to each other. In the maid's room I found Rosalind not only awake but standing by the lamp, holding my handwritten note under the light and trying to read it.

'Christ!' she yipped, startled.

'You all right?'

She put down the note and seemed for the first time to see the ratty dressing gown she was wearing. 'Of course,' she said in a vaguely irritated tone. 'Where the hell am I?'

'Jane Tait's apartment.'

'Mind telling me why?' Her voice had an edge to it.

'You don't remember?'

'Max, start making sense.'

I shook my head in awe. The stuff they'd fed her was prime, all right. 'Do you remember a fight you had in my room at Blue's?'

She stood motionless for a long time, her big dark eyes fixed on me, her hair tousled, but still attractive. I found myself wondering what it would take to really muss her up. 'Angie,' she said then.

'What?'

'That little bastard, Angie. He hit me.'

'You remember that.'

The look of pain that was never far below the surface of her face now emerged like a cloud, shadowing her eyes and the hollows under her cheekbones. 'Please, Max, stop making me guess.'

'He shot you full of something remarkable,' I told her. 'Some drug that had you sleeping like a baby for damned near —' I glanced at my watch. 'Twelve hours.'

'Why?'

'You don't remember the steamer trunk?'

'Max!'

'He stashed you in a trunk. I think the idea was to export you fast. You were supposed to wake up on the Continent, unless,' I added, feeling a cold shiver of sympathy, 'you woke inside the trunk, that is.'

She made a gagging noise in her throat, then pulled the wrapper around her. We stood watching each other. I didn't know what to suggest next, but I didn't have to. She yawned once, a small, ladylike movement. Then came a bigger yawn. She sat down on the bed and gave me a helpless look.

'Obviously the stuff hasn't all worn off.' I went to the bed and eased her head back on the pillow. 'We'll talk about it in the morning.'

'Mm?' Her eyelids flickered. Then they closed over the great dark eyes.

Her breathing grew regular and deep. I tiptoed out of the room and went to the kitchen. Jane Tait wasn't there but all the glasses and plates had been stacked neatly in the sink. I went looking for my hostess.

She had already gone to bed. In the darkness of her room she sat up, holding the sheets to her breast. 'Your room's down the hall,' she said, 'next to Sleeping Beauty. She's finally awake, I gather.'

'Went back to sleep.'

'Good night then.' She lay back.

'Can I talk to you?'

'In the morning.' She sounded annoyed.

'Thank you for everything,' I said, starting to let myself out of her room.

'In the morning.'

I found the room that was supposed to be mine, undressed and got in the narrow single bed. My watch told me it was nearly three a.m. I closed my eyes and was asleep almost at once.

Almost at once I was awake. Someone was slipping into my bed, someone small with long, dark hair, who had first removed an ancient flowered dressing gown. I checked my watch. Three-thirty a.m.

'Roz,' I began, 'this bed's too small f —'

'Shut up. I was freezing in there.' She got in with her back to me, arranged my arms around her and then curled into a foetal position with me as a wrapper. 'Like two spoons in a drawer,' she murmured, wriggling against me, skin on skin.

By four-thirty, evidently, she had generated enough body heat to get up and return to her own bed. In addition to playing spoons, what she'd had in mind was really too awkward for a narrow bed. However, we managed. As always, when it was over, she had the same effect on me: insomnia.

I lay there for a long time, wondering why I couldn't seem to work up any great amount of enthusiasm for my situation.

Earlier today – Saturday, that is; 'today' was now Sunday – I had reached a point where I was ready to opt out. What I do can't be done well when someone has me under surveillance. It's not impossible, it just takes a lot more effort and, of course, runs to a lot more risk.

That the curly-headed fellow with the red sweater was on my tail could not be argued away. Inept or not, he'd been assigned to follow me.

I got out of bed, pulling on a man's robe that had been laid on the chaise longue in my temporary room. I wondered where Jane Tait had come by such a robe – a bit too small for me, but adequate. When I got to the kitchen I had a chance to find out. She was awake, standing at the stove and stirring something in a pot.

'Whose robe is this?'

She didn't flinch or jump. She merely turned slowly, looking taller than she usually did, even though her feet were bare. She had put on what must have been her absolutely smashing best dressing gown, a green-and-gold affair like sunlight through a jungle.

'Do you want some chocolate?'

'Yes, thank you. Can't you sleep either?'

'These old flats produce strange noises at night.'

She delivered this in such a dry tone that I realized she'd been able to hear Roz and me trying to build up her body heat. 'Did that keep you awake?'

'It awakened me,' she corrected. 'Then it kept me awake.'

'Whose robe is this?' I countered.

'Do you like your cocoa very sweet?'

'Not too.' I stood behind her, watching her stir the milk to keep it from boiling. 'Can I ask you a personal question?'

'Why not?'

'It's multiple-choice.'

'How very American.'

'Choose the response that most closely approximates your feelings,' I reeled off. 'A. You are not angry with me at all. B. You are angry, but you are saving it for a big explosion later. C. You will never tell me how you feel because you think you have to cater to me as a valuable property of your publishing house.'

She continued stirring for a moment, then shut off the gas and quickly poured two mugfuls. 'None of the above,' she said, handing me my hot chocolate.

We sat on opposite sides of her kitchen table staring at each other over the steam rising from our mugs. 'You don't play fair,' I said.

'Nor do you.' With one hand she fidgeted open a metal box of cookies. 'Have one?'

I shook my head. 'Tell me.'

'Well.' She bit into a cookie and left a neat crescent. 'First, I don't believe I have to cater to you because you're one of Ian's big selling authors.' She studied the bitten cookie. 'Even though I'll admit I have been catering quite a bit to you. No, it's not infatuation, either.' She laid down the half-bitten cookie and picked up a fresh one. 'Not camaraderie. Not lust.' She sighed. 'I guess it's the feeling one has for a stray. You're a stray, Max. You operate alone in a world where everyone needs help. Especially strays. You really have no idea how dangerous a life it is. I'm only now beginning to appreciate bits and pieces of it.'

She sipped her cocoa and continued musing out loud, almost as if she were by herself in the kitchen. 'At first I thought, well, this is one of those very American *macho* things. Lookit me,' she said lasping into a really bad Western drawl, 'Ah'm a gunna steal all thuh money and fuck all thuh wimmen.' She bit into the new cookie, thus producing a second half-moon remainder. 'But that isn't your way. You don't need an audience. What you do is masturbatory, it's for yourself. You may not want it that way, but you choose courses of action that of necessity remain unseen.' She started to bite into a third cookie, but stopped and looked up at me. 'All that would be consistent, if nothing else,' she told me. 'But then you write books about it. That's neither a passion nor secrecy, nor narcissist posturing. It's a plain old death wish.'

'Is it?'

'Max,' she said, her words suddenly rushed with urgency. 'That woman is bad news. She carries such an aura of trouble that—'

'I know it.'

'Drugged and shipped in a trunk? I mean, dear God, I ask you.'

'Like common baggage,' I agreed. 'You don't have to be jealous of her, Emma Jane. There really isn't any feeling going in either direction.'

She gave me a pained look. 'Don't reduce this to something personal and petty, Max. I'm not giving you advice from a position as a wronged woman.'

'Right. You'll be pleased to know that I'm turning her back to her gangster friend. On one point you and I agree completely; this thing is getting too rich for my blood.'

'Turn her back? He'll destroy her.'

'No, he loves her.'

'You can't do that to her, Max.' Her blue-grey-green eyes looked like jade at the moment, hard stony eyes that disapproved of me completely.

'This is not a game of finders-keepers.'

Jane Tait glanced at her kitchen clock and so did I. It was nearly five in the morning. 'You can't do that,' she repeated again, 'because it would be the lowest kind of treachery.'

'I thought you didn't like her.'

A sharp gasp of annoyance escaped her. She stood up and padded on bare feet to the kitchen window, folded her arms over her breasts and stared out into the darkness. 'You brought her here,' she said, evidently having some trouble keeping her voice down. 'You were on a spot. You had rescued her and you needed a hiding place. I didn't suggest my place. You commandeered it. You felt strongly enough about it yesterday to do all that to protect her. The moment the woman regains consciousness, you start making plans to betray her.'

'But she can't stay here.'

'Where can she go?' She turned towards me, arms still folded. 'Start behaving like a human being, Max. There was a moment yesterday when you gave a convincing imitation. I don't like her. But she's in trouble.'

'It may only be through Monday morning,' I suggested, remembering when the time locks opened at the bank vault. 'I'm sorry I got you into this.'

'You? Sorry?'

'This isn't your world,' I said. 'And this certainly isn't your scene, hot and cold running brunettes in your beds.'

Her mouth flattened into a perfectly horizontal line. 'I'm not getting through to you at all, am I Max?' She left the window and stood in front of me now. 'You're keeping me at arm's length, the way you keep everybody.'

'That's for your own good, Emma Jane.'

She took the cup of cocoa out of my hands and put it on the table. 'You get a lot of mileage out of that line, don't you. But actually, you don't like people getting close to you.'

'Um.'

She took my hand and pulled me to my feet. 'Let's try and get some sleep. Come to bed.'

Hers was double size. I tried the spoons thing but Jane Tait was too tall. Still and all, I slept. Finally.

CHAPTER SEVENTEEN

At nine in the morning, I woke Jane Tait long enough to get the key to her publisher's office. Then I returned to my hotel.

The room had been completely put to rights. I changed clothes, shaved and went down to the desk with a key to the safe-deposit box I'd rented on arrival. The hundred dollar bills were there, and a few other things.

A different desk clerk was on duty, so there was no point in asking him any clever questions about a young man who'd been assaulted on their loading platform. I also wanted to know about their cleaning ladies. Instead, I simply took out one folded bit of cardboard and watched him return the lock box to its drawer. Nothing in his utterly controlled manner indicated a burning desire to know how my room had got so chewed up the day before. There is a lot to be said for British reticence.

I suppose it's inevitable in a society as money-oriented as ours that all sorts of things are for sale if the price is right. We need so many strange things. It's to be expected that someone, an organization, will be in business to supply what we want.

A man with two speeding violations on his driver's licence will have it taken away if he's caught a third time. He will pay – these are East Coast US prices – five hundred dollars to have a brand new licence which is supplied on official stock stolen from the printer who supplies the state motor-vehicle bureau. For a thousand dollars more, someone will break into the computer room of the bureau, find the tape on which the customer's speeding violations are recorded and wipe it clean with an electromagnet.

Bizarre needs. Someone has been recklessly incautious, takes Polaroids at an orgy, leaves the photos where an employee finds them. It's too risky to make a direct blackmail play. The employee brokers the photos through an organization adept at such things. Services, Unlimited.

Is it any wonder, then, that I can buy a perfectly good, new passport in the name of anyone at all, complete with proper photo? Or that I can buy something like the folded piece of plasticized cardboard I had removed from the lock box?

It shows that I am a Captain Paul Phelps in United States Army Intelligence, on duty assignment to the National Intelligence Agency in Virginia. The picture is of me, but badly lighted. I also have a card indicating that I am a sergeant in the New York Police Department Intelligence Division. Hard to tell what I do for them. Maybe I chase down forged documents.

Armed with my Captain Phelps card, I set out on foot for the US Embassy in Grosvenor Square.

I felt a little better this morning than I had the previous evening. Then I'd just been pulling myself together after discovering that I was under someone's surveillance. I'd been suffering the luxury of thinking I had the option of bowing out.

Then after Jane Tait's mini-lecture on loyalty, I realized I was well and truly mired in it and there was no turning back. It's amazing how desperation dispels anxiety. No, really. When there is a chance of turning back the agony of making the decision is acute. Once you've no choice, you relax and enjoy it.

But there was no point in relaxing into carelessness. I left Blue's on foot, primarily to see if I'd picked up a tail. I hadn't spotted any from Jane Tait's to the hotel, but I'd been in a cab. Now was the time I'd see what surfaced.

He did. No red sweater this time. Curly blond hair, cut

short. Very nice Sunday-stroll outfit, light grey trousers, dark blue blazer, striped dress shirt open at the neck. Boyish. I stood at the corner of Piccadilly and St James's and watched out of the corner of my eye as he hopped into a dark grey Austin Mini.

I began to wonder what the hell I was watching.

First the red sweater, a capital mistake. Now the idea of using a car to follow a man on foot. Perhaps he'd used it to follow me from Jane Tait's, but now was the time to ditch it. It slowly, slowly dawned on me why he kept the car. Living with two women had addled my mind, especially after last night, when the sleeping arrangements had been, to put it politely, erratic.

It began to percolate through my head that the man in the Mini was nothing more or less than a green boy.

He was Uncle's, and he wasn't very experienced. Nobody had thought it necessary to warn him about red sweaters or following a pedestrian in a car. As a matter of fact, the two clowns in the grey Ford who had tailed Dorani from La Place had made the same mistake.

It's a peculiarly American mistake. We tend to think that if anyone's in motion, he's in a car. Some of us still haven't learned the European style of walking to places. If we're assigned a subject to tail, we automatically resort to a wheeled vehicle.

I crossed Piccadilly and headed directly into Berkeley Street, which went the wrong way for the man in the Mini. This wasn't so much to shake him as to test what he'd do next. If he abandoned the Mini and took to shoeleather, then he was worthy of some respect. Otherwise . . .

When he failed to reappear, on or off wheels, I decided he was an exceedingly recent graduate of spy school. It would be a mistake to think all Uncle's beginners are that inept. Some bring a certain amount of built-in expertise, especially when they're recruited from the ranks of organized crime, as many are. But this lad didn't just seem inexperienced, he seemed stupid.

Gradually, as I crossed Berkeley Square and walked along Mount Street towards Grosvenor Square, the expected reaction set in. What did Uncle mean, assigning such an inept operative to a hot shot like me? Had my name sunk that low on the enemies list? Did Uncle think that years of writing novels and living the good life had dulled my other abilities? The nerve of Uncle!

It was enough of a slight to start me wondering just how rusty I'd got at this sort of thing. That is what I was wondering, in fact, as I came to Carlos Place and followed it to the edge of Grosvenor Square. The Embassy stood diagonally across the green from me. I stepped into Grosvenor Street, watching the way the April breeze fluttered the Stars and Stripes.

The grey Mini was doing about sixty miles an hour. It whipped around the corner with a moan of disk brakes and started to run me down.

I catapulted forward, the kind of dive one usually does off the edge of a swimming pool, knowing one's going into water. I dropped headlong on the cobblestones and skidded a foot or so.

That was what saved me, that extra foot of skid. The Mini's left front wheel actually clipped the toe of my shoe as it roared past.

I only had time to crane my neck after it, to see it swerve wildly out of sight around the corner of Adam's Row. The boy behind the wheel downshifted in a howl of gears. The sound grew distant.

Then silence.

CHAPTER EIGHTEEN

The porter who normally opened the publisher's office was not to be found. I let myself into the building with Jane's key and went to my cubbyhole to listen to the sound of drilling over the FM receiver. I sat there, rubbing my sore knees and contemplating the tip of my right shoe, scraped clean of polish where it had violently pressed down across the cobblestones. I also listened to some of the most industrious lads in London. Marvellous what money can buy in the way of hard work.

I wondered if they'd worked all night. They seemed to have an inexhaustible supply of rock-cutting bits. Every ten minutes or so the drill stopped for a while to let them fit a replacement. I tried to judge by the sound if they were any closer to breaking in, but couldn't make up my mind.

Switching off the receiver, I left the building and presented myself inside the US Embassy. The duty clerk behind the lobby counter this Sunday was too low in rank for what I had in mind.

'But there's no one else in today,' he assured me.

I shook my head in a mysterious fashion, as if I knew whereof I spoke. 'I am not allowed to open up this can of worms to anyone below an assistant consular aide.' I flashed the Army Intelligence card at him.

He picked up a phone and consulted someone. When he hung up he indicated a stairway to the left. 'The door at the head of the stairs. He's expecting you.'

The consular aide looked to be in his mid-twenties. He inspected my identification and his face grew grave.

'What can we do for you, Captain Phelps?'

'Just a routine inquiry,' I began in the classic mode. 'It doesn't indicate anything derogatory about its subject. You understand.'

'Of course.'

'Does the name David Bushnell Greeley ring a bell?'

He repeated the name silently, lips moving, then wrote it down. 'No.'

'He's an American citizen living in London. We want to interview him but he isn't at any of his known addresses.'

'There's no reason why we should have any inf —'

'Um, there may be,' I cut in. 'Greeley was CIA until a few years ago.'

He gave me a look of hurt shock, as if remonstrating with me for getting him involved this carefree Sunday in something he wanted to stay out of. 'Defector?'

'Nothing like that. We just want to talk to him. We thought your files-people might be about to produce some addresses we don't have. Or names of friends and associates.'

'Our files?' He looked suddenly relieved. 'Files are closed on Sunday, Captain. I'm very much afraid —' a big grin flashed on his face for a moment at the thought that he could buck this problem to someone else. '— you'll have to come back tomorrow morning. Can it wait that long?'

'It'll have to.' I was on my feet. 'Shall I ask for you?'

'No, no, no. The files department will be open. Apply directly to Miss Hudder.'

'Miss Hudder. Thank you.'

We shook hands. I left but, instead of coming down the stairs, I slipped to the end of the corridor nearest the Manhattan Bank and Trust Company and descended the flight of stairs there. They led to another flight. Walking downstairs hurt my knees, but I kept moving.

In a moment I was in the basement, moving in the direction of Grosvenor Square until I estimated I was directly in line with the bank vault around the corner.

What I was looking at, instead, was an ordinary wooden door marked 'Files'. It was locked. I loided it open and found myself in a room that extended even closer towards the common wall with the bank. File drawers five high lined all the sides and stood in the centre of the room. I moved towards the common wall.

As I did so, I could begin to hear the faint hum of a drill, thin as a faraway mosquito, but familiar enough. I moved slowly towards the sound. That was how I found myself looking at the closed door of a vault only a bit smaller than the Diebold on the other side of the wall.

The tunnellers were inside the US Embassy's vault. What better cover for the noise? The vault was probably timed to open at nine-thirty a.m. Monday, but perhaps the people inside had put an override on the mechanism to let them out whenever they wanted.

It didn't make sense. I'd never heard of being able to override the time-release mechanisms of these big vaults. Still, there were all sorts of tricks to this trade.

I backed away and tiptoed towards the outer door, marked 'Files'. The Embassy people upstairs would be looking for me by now. It was time to be limping along on my bruised legs. But I paused for a moment at the desk there, which was when I found out how they planned to override the time-lock. They weren't.

At nine-thirty a.m. Monday they would simply wait for the release to open the door and boldly walk out past the head of Files Department. According to the placard on her desk, she was a Miss Hudder.

A Miss Clarissa Hudder. Dave Greeley's Clarissa?

CHAPTER NINETEEN

They were sitting at Jane Tait's dining-room table, two heads together, almost touching, dark blonde and sable black. Rosalind Rue was slowly turning the pages of her scrapbook and pointing to things. The time was nearly noon, but neither of them seemed to have had anything except coffee.

'Thinking of publishing the scrapbook?' I asked Jane Tait.

'If only we could.'

She stared at me for a long moment. 'What have you done to your trouser knees?' Her eyes were sharper than the embassy clerk's.

I dusted them off again, neglecting to mention what I'd done to the human knees inside. 'How's the patient?' I asked Roz.

She looked up at me then with the full load of pain in her face. She drew the edges of Jane Tait's flowered wrapper closer around her and tried a slight smile.

'I wasn't making much sense when I came out of it. Did you really find me in a steamer trunk?'

'You really don't remember, do you?'

'I remember Angie chopping at the back of my neck.' Her hand reached around under the thick black curls of hair to cradle the area directly behind her right ear. 'We had a terrible row in your room.' Her glance shifted from me to Jane Tait, as if assuring herself that it was all right to admit having been in my room. Any of my rooms.

'Is he one of Moe's bodyguards?'

She nodded. 'The other must be with Moey on the continent.'

'If that's where he went.' I sat down and poured myself some coffee, for all the world like a character in a daytime television soap opera who is forever talking, talking, at someone's kitchen table.

'Let me describe a fella to you. Twenty-seven or so, five-ten, curly blond hair, light eyes. Nice looking, good dresser. Work for Moe?'

She frowned. 'Doesn't ring a bell. Angie is dark with black-black eyes.'

I nodded. 'Like ripe olives.'

'Exactly.'

'And the one you think is with him on the Continent?'

'Fiftyish, ex-pug. Squashed ear.'

I nodded. Curly wasn't Moe's boy. He had to be Uncle's.

'Have you had a chance to decide why Foxy Grandpa wanted you shipped abroad in a crate?' I asked then.

'Does it have to be Moey? Couldn't Angie have been working for someone else?'

I hadn't thought of that. This lady seemed to know her way around the mores and customs of organized crime. Like anything else dedicated to making money, the mob propounded magnificent rules and regulations which it systematically violated at every opportunity. Honour among thieves is about as credible a concept as honour among politicians.

So even though Angie might be bound by strong ties of loyalty to Moe Gordon, there always existed the chance that he might be suborned, or pressured, into betraying his master, if only to the extent of kidnapping the man's protégé.

'Do you honestly think Moe didn't know?' I countered then. 'Maybe he's waiting across the Channel right now, waiting to take delivery.' When she shook her head, I tried another idea. 'Who is big enough to override Moe's control over Angie?'

She shook her head again, not with lack of understanding, but with the idea that there were too many people and too many ways Moe Gordon could be under-cut. It was a fresh concept for me. I wanted to know more.

'Lately, you know,' she began, 'all these Senate hearings ...' Her voice died away. I glanced at Jane Tait and saw that she was as rapt as I in what the actress was saying.

'You mean Moe Gordon's rear end is exposed? What could a bunch of senators have on him that nobody else has been able to make stick for forty years?'

The look of pain deepened to anguish. She brushed back her hair as she bent forward to sip coffee. 'I don't know,' she said then. Her dark glance swept from Jane Tait to me. 'I just want out of this. I want to pick up my career, whatever's left. I want to stop being somebody's moll.'

'What makes you think Moe's in trouble? He comes on strong as always,' I said. 'He's locked in some high-level deal right now with his opposite number in the Union Corse. Dorani?'

There was no recognition in Rosalind's eyes. 'I know almost nothing about what Moey does,' she said in a small voice.

'Besides the movie business, that is.'

She blushed. 'I still want that part, Max.'

'You haven't seen any signs he's running scared? People not answering his phone calls? People refusing to meet him? Strange accidents?'

'Accidents?' She stared into my eyes? 'Why did you say that?'

'There's been a car accident recently?'

'It wasn't in the papers. How did y —?'

I sat back and surveyed the two women, wondering whether we weren't long past the point where I had to be circumspect with them. What I was about to say would only alarm them, but it might trigger Roz to remember more.

'Does the name Murray Chotiner mean anything to you?' I asked then. Neither responded.

'He was a syndicate lawyer assigned to handle Nixon's political campaigns. Remarkable tactician. Had to know all the names, dates, places, sums of money. The man was a walking time-bomb of confidential information. Even had a private office in the White House. But when the strategy was to make Nixon into a global statesman, Chotiner had to go. The German High Command – Kissinger, Ehrlichman, Haldeman and the rest – eased him out of the White House, literally. Unlike other long-time apparatniks like Rebozo, Chotiner was not a fat cat. He was just a lawyer who'd lost his clout and had to scramble for a living.

'One afternoon he drove to Senator Teddy Kennedy's home near Washington, D.C. We don't know if he was trying to peddle information or what. They ran him down with a rented truck, typical Mafia m.o., but only gave him a broken leg and a slight concussion. It was Teddy who called the ambulance for him. Chotiner did very well in the hospital and was to be discharged a few days later. Over night, he died ... of an embolism. That's something in the blood that reaches the tiny brain capillaries and causes death. Something like an air bubble.'

Neither woman said anything. I cleared my throat. 'The first weapon of choice was the rented truck. Once you had your man in a hospital bed, the backup weapon would be the Sicilian Air Bubble. Were you with Moe Gordon when his car got hit by a rented truck?'

Her full, wide mouth, devoid of lipstick, was chalky. Her lips formed and reformed silent syllables. Then, shakily: 'A Ford van. Just the other side of the George Washington Bridge, where you get on to Interstate 80. The van came out of Highway 4 and hit Moey's car right into the door next to him. Then it backed up and escaped along Highway 4.'

'He didn't report it.'

'Of course not.'

'Do you know why?'

'Moe doesn't deal with the police.'

'Wrong,' I told her. 'He recognized who had sent the van. He didn't report it because he didn't want the world to know he was slated for a Chotiner exit.'

Jane Tait frowned. 'I don't understand. When a man's been that important for that length of time, he's too dangerous to *try* to kill. One would surely have only one guaranteed crack at Moe Gordon. Poison or something.'

'These mechanics are never fool-proof with a truck or car,' I said. 'But even if they only injured him, they'd administer the coup de grâce in the hospital.'

'But why?' Roz burst out.

'I think Jane said it. When a man's been that important for that length of time, he had to die. If only to bury what he knows with him.'

'A lot of his friends live to a ripe old age.'

'Not when they achieve national prominence,' I demurred. 'Your true mobster stays out of the headlines. But Moe Gordon has always had a weakness for celebrity. Either because of that, or by arrangement with his business partners, he's been Mr Front Man ever since the Second World War. It was a good move, making this kindly old grandpa into a trademark, but in the highest circles of respect there would always be the thought that Moe wasn't totally serious.'

'That's no reason to kill him,' Jane Tait pointed out.

She had a point. There were one or two other old men who knew as much as Moe Gordon. Nobody was ramming their limousines or kidnapping their mistresses. Yet. There had to be something more and, if Roz were right, it had to do with the Senate investigations.

'Why did you pinpoint the Senate thing?' I asked her.

'It was just after the hearing opened that he bundled us off to London.'

'He could still be extradited to testify.'

I started to ask a question and stopped. I don't often do that. I had wanted to ask about the handwriting in her scrapbook under the photo of President Kennedy. Normally the mob has no politics. It backs whoever can win.

CHAPTER TWENTY

I don't know how sultans and other noted polygamists do it. Living with one woman is always something of a trial. Living with two doesn't double the trouble, it forces one into binds one never knew existed.

For instance, over the weekend, what about clothes? I mean, none of Jane Tait's clothing fitted Roz Rue. And Roz couldn't be expected to slop around in a sleazy wrapper, now could she? And the shops were closed on Sunday. And eating? Why should Jane Tait turn herself into a kitchen slavey? Couldn't we all go out for a nice afternoon dinner? What about the Hungry Horse on Fulham Road? What about not letting anyone see Roz or else we might all be put away permanently in steamer trunks? But this was a shameful waste of a Sunday. One couldn't be expected to sit around reading the papers and waiting for something to show up on the telly. And Jane Tait wasn't running a flophouse after all. Then, too, she really didn't want a repetition of last night's catch-as-catch-can sleeping arrangements.

What finally happened Sunday night was that, like a coward, I went back to Blue's Hotel. I was a bit apprehensive about what might happen between the two women in my absence, not because they were hostile to each other but only because they were both cooped up, bored and much put upon by the vagaries of fate. Jane was being very civil, but her conversation was getting a terribly clipped tone.

I had no idea what awaited me at Blue's. Whoever the brain was behind the attempted export of Roz's body would now be back at work trying to figure out what went wrong, and inevitably coming up with the name of Max Patrick. The young fellow with the ripe olive eyes whom I had kneed into oblivion would certainly now be among the ambulatory and eagerly searching for the owner of the knee. The blond lad with the Austin Mini would likely be back, too, unless his boss had shrewdly substituted a new agent.

So when I approached the desk Sunday evening and asked for messages, I was prepared for almost anything, even perhaps a letter that exploded when I opened it.

But I was not prepared for what was in fact waiting there for me: a small, almost square envelope of heavy taupe stock with flowing script initials embossed on the back flap. They were so flowing, in fact, that I couldn't actually make them out. A G, perhaps, and a W? Or was it an H?

The letter seemed too flat to hold a bomb so I cracked open the flap and withdrew a folded note on the same taupe paper with the same indecipherable monogram.

'Mr Patrick,' it began in one of those backhand writing styles, with a tiny circle instead of a dot over the i, 'Dave G. desperately needs your help. Please come to him at any hour.' There followed an address on Sangrail Close in Chelsea off Cheyne Walk, where the Embankment runs along the river. It was the area known as World's End. I'd never been there. The note was signed C. Hudder.

I put it back in its envelope, asked the clerk for a larger one, enclosed Clarissa Hudder's letter in the Blue's Hotel envelope and sealed it. On the outside I wrote 'To be opened by Jane Tait', and gave it back to the desk clerk to put in my message box.

As I returned to my room I tried to think of next steps. My mind refused to cope, but instead messed about with non-clues, such as the fact that the monogram had undoubtedly been a C and an H.

I let myself into the room and made certain no one was hiding there. Then I sat down on the sofa and tried to think. It was obvious that the reason I was having so little luck was that my mind was shying away from a central fact: I would have to go to World's End.

I didn't want to. Everything I know of life told me it was a set-up. Clarissa Hudder was not a good guy. She and Dave were bad guys or, at least, in the hands of bad guys. Since she was in charge of the Embassy's files, she was undoubtedly a CIA plant Dave had first known in the days when he, too, served The Outfit.

Whoever had dreamed up the looting of the Manhattan Bank's vault trusted Dave Greeley even less than I did. He wasn't part of the master plan. At the moment of action, he had been lured away and replaced by a double.

Was it too much to assume they'd done the same with Miss Hudder? As I have mentioned earlier in these pages, finding a reliable *doppelgänger* isn't any cinch. Finding two of them, including a woman who had to know the files and her CIA routine as well, seemed far too difficult.

Unless the prize was worth it.

Sitting in my darkened room, alone, frankly funking my next move, I tried to imagine what could be in the Manhattan's vault that would be worth all this man-oeuvring and substitution, not forgetting the involvement of Moe Gordon in it.

In any event, was I actually dumb enough to go some-place where I was expected? Where the lad in the Mini could do the job right this time?

But ... there were considerations.

What Rosalind Rue had told me earlier – that her Moey was in trouble with his own people – cast a new light on everything. An affiliated mobster operating a certificate Syndicate scam is one thing. He's the most protected hood on earth. Not even the Pope in Rome can touch him. But let him lose the confidence of his confrères and he's elevated rapidly to Number One on the Hit Parade.

How could I, from the outside, decide who was doing what to whom? Had Moe Gordon bought Dave Greeley?

CHAPTER TWENTY-ONE

I didn't find Sangrail Close at once.

This part of London, at the far end of Chelsea, is not easy for an outsider to know. There is a World's End Passage, of course, a sort of cul-de-sac of trendy flats. There is the Cremorne Establishment – was it kin to the pleasure park where Victorian blades paid naked slaveys to birch them?

It's an odd part of town, in a strange way that is difficult to explain, except perhaps by the proximity of the river. Dusk had fallen some time before I reached World's End. The cab driver wasn't sure where I wanted to be let off and neither was I. I didn't want to give him the name of Sangrail Close. The fewer witnesses connecting me to whatever was lying ahead, the better. Jane Tait, opening the letter I'd left for her, would have the key, if a key were needed later.

As is often true of April, the weather had grown chilly once the sun was down. Wisps of fog lifted off the river's fast-flowing surface. After a few minutes of searching for Sangrail Close, the cold had got in my bones and I shivered.

There were damned few precautions one could take on such a mission. I don't carry guns. They make me nervous, as they should any thinking person, because guns end up doing one's thinking for one.

If I were faced with something that, at the instant, I couldn't think through with my brain, carrying a gun would at once suggest another solution. In its shoulder holster or on the hip, a gun radiated a kind of dumb menace that, for all its being only steel and brass, could overwhelm the mind of the person who carried it.

By branching into the sideline I had chosen, I had picked a relatively non-violent profession, or so it had seemed at the beginning. Yet there had been times when I'd longed like the lowest moron for a gun. Now was one of those times.

I wondered if Jack Philemon carried a gun. Probably only on demand. Perhaps tonight would have been a good time to hire him. And his gun.

I was blundering along Cheyne Walk again, moving away from the neat little slice of greenery where it branches off from the Chelsea Embankment. The darkness of the night seemed emphasized by the growing mist that put around each street lamp a pearly nimbus. Traffic was sparse, but the headlights of cars looked huge in the fog, like the feral eyes of stalking animals.

I was standing, for the third time around, where Beaufort Street crosses Cheyne Walk and becomes the Battersea Bridge over the Thames. On the other side of the river the lights of Battersea Park had begun to disappear in the growing fog. In a moment, I heard the first of the horns, moaning in protest.

It occurred to me that if I'd created the scene for a novel, it would have been too hokey for most readers. Night. Fog. Thames shrouded in mist. Ghostly moan of fog-horns. Unknown destination. Unknowable menace. Too bloody thick, right?

For me, too, as I tried a new way into World's End. Success, at last. A passageway no wider than a yard, which I had bypassed before, now seemed likely. High up on the brick of a building I saw the sign I'd missed for Sangrail Close. I moved slowly. No sense rushing into what was a set-up designed exclusively for Max Patrick, Esq.

Clarissa Hudder's backslanting handwriting, very Wellesley or Vassar in the style preferred by women students of about fifteen years ago, had given the address as Number Five, with another of her tiny circles over the i.

As far as I could tell, Sangrail Close was not really open to the sky. The buildings on either side, grimy brick sweating moisture in the fog, seemed to close together and meet over my head. I passed a Number One and a Number Three, mere doorways, before the passage widened slightly into a kind of diamond shape several yards across.

Number Five had its own staircase, five steps of white-washed stone that led to a Georgian door, scarlet in the glow of two brass sidelamps, with an ornate fanlight above it of cut-crystal panes. The massive brass knocker was cast in the shape of a lion's face, more human than animal, lips pulled back in a rictus of rage, fangs bared for a hungry bite.

An oval lozenge of brass had been set into the door below the lion's head but its surface was absolutely smooth. No name had been engraved there. I lifted the lion by his chin and banged him twice against the plate. The knocking sound was a mere rap. There was no resonance to the door, telling me it was quite thick, perhaps reinforced, certainly bullet-proof.

With no telltale footsteps sounding from behind it, the lock produced a cushioned click and the door swung open. A man stood there whom I had seen before, but couldn't remember where. He was short, wide through the shoulders, with almost no neck and arms so long his fingertips almost reached his kneecaps. He smiled very nicely.

'*Bon soir*, M'sieur Potreek,' he murmured.

I made him then, one of the two associates who had flown from New York with Jean-Luc Dorani. I tried to return the smile, but there was simply no comparison between my average medium-white front teeth, some capped, some real, and No-Neck's glorious gold crowns, all eight of them.

'Is Mr Dorani expecting me?' I asked.

'This way, sir.'

Although the four-storey house had been well furnished in the Georgian period to match its front door, the place had an air of impermanence about it. Not enough pictures on the walls? Too few chairs? Something motel-room about it created the atmosphere of a place of passage, like the mysterious close outside, where rare birds alighted from time to time on great flights from one faraway corner of the world to another.

Jean-Luc Dorani was waiting for me in a neat parlour to the left of the entrance hall. A fire crackled fitfully in the hearth, giving off as much smoke as heat in the humid atmosphere. I say Dorani was waiting for me. Actually, he had staged the confrontation so that I seemed to be an afterthought he'd almost forgotten.

His thin, elegant frame was half hidden in an immense wingback chair. On his lap sat one of those leather zipper cases that opens into a letter writing kit. He had been hard at work on some abstruse calculation for which he also used a small electronic calculator.

He punched up an equation, noted the result and copied it with a fountain pen on to his worksheet. The proper titan of business number continued through one more calculation until he looked up, 'saw' me and, with a great show of hospitality, put aside his letter case and calculator before getting to his feet.

We shook hands, his fingers almost exactly like steel rods that clamped down on mine as if to brand a permanent impression there. In a way, I suppose, they did. Then, seeing me to be a head taller, he sat down again.

'You are kind to come,' he said in precise but strangely accented English. There was a lingering half-breath of a syllable after 'kind', as if he had once conquered an Italian accent and no longer put feminine endings on consonants just because something inside felt better if he did.

'If I had known who my host would be,' I said, sitting in an exact duplicate of his chair across the hearth from him, 'I would have been here much sooner. Forgive my delay.'

A pained look crossed his face. 'I only just got here myself,' he explained, re-establishing the pecking order.

He sat quietly for a moment, watching. His face, with its sharp nose, was narrow through the jaw, which gave him a hungry look he probably knew was fearsome. He rarely smiled, therefore. His dark hair had begun to recede, giving the top of his face a strangely intellectual cast, as of a professor with some terribly important matters to consider.

Still not risking a smile, Dorani allowed the corners of his mouth to quirk upwards faintly, an I'm-not-going-to-eat you signal I didn't for a moment believe. 'You are, of course, known to me, Mr Patrick.'

'Favourably?'

'I have read your books in the French Gallimard editions. Most amusing.'

He let the corners of his mouth rest for a moment. Then abruptly they turned down and his chin came up at the same time his hands turned palms up and moved slightly away from each other in an I-have-no-choice gesture.

'But it isn't through your books that we first met,' he said in a darker voice. 'It is through the events of life.'

'I wasn't aware th —'

'No, of course you weren't,' he cut in. 'At Dubrovnik you naturally assumed you were alone. That no eye had followed the moves.' He made a sound like a stifled laugh. 'Which made your novel about it all the more amusing. Tell me, why did you change the gold chalice to a glass krater in the book?'

'A matter of literary licence.'

'Please explain.'

He had slanted eyes with the heavy lids that make a man look sleepy when, in fact, he is anything but. Moorish? Perhaps a heritage of some Saracen raider during the Dark Ages. To have Dorani's eyes upon one was an extraordinary experience in the sense that, whether one lied or not, the feeling was that every stratagem was seen through.

'Gold is only a commodity,' I explained. 'Even a chalice of beautiful Scythian workmanship, worth perhaps half a million dollars on the legitimate market, doesn't quite have the, um, cachet of something as unknown as a krater of antique glass with the patina of twenty-five centuries upon it. The average reader knows all about gold. But he is in awe of something as foreign to his experience as the krater. Also, of course, I didn't want to implicate the Kunstmuseum which bought the chalice. You under stand.'

'Delicate work. I understand.'

'Even more delicate to have seen all this and not to have interfered.'

Dorani acknowledged the compliment with a grave nod. 'Until now, that is,' he added then.

'Is there something you want of me?'

This time only one corner of his mouth quirked up. 'There is something I don't want of you,' he said after a moment. 'Just as there is something you don't want of me.'

'I'm not sure I —'

'You want me to do nothing about Dubrovnik. It was only a few years ago. The statute of limitations ...' He let the thought die. 'In return, I want you to do nothing also.'

'About what?'

'Let me put it to you in a positive manner, Mr Patrick.' He leaned forward so that the firelight made his slanted eyes glitter. 'I want you to stay *out* of the Grosvenor Square business.'

'The —?'

'There will be no deceptions between us. Stay out of the Files department of the Embassy. Stay out of the Manhattan Bank's vault. I don't ask you to leave London. I don't *tell* you to leave London. I want you only to do

nothing. Nothing.' His mouth turned down at the sides.
'Nothing,' he repeated.

'In return for your doing nothing about Dubrovnik?'

'Exactly.'

'I agree, on one condition.'

His face went dead as he leaned back into the depths
of the wing chair. 'You agree, period.'

'*Sensa dubbio*,' I said, slipping into Italian because I
was too rattled to speak in French. 'But let's not call it
a condition, then. Call it a favour from a man powerful
enough to grant such a favour.'

His posture eased. Some of the starch seemed to go out
of him. I had been idiotic to demand a 'condition'. A
'favour' he understood. 'What is the favour Mr Patrick?'

'That you give me some idea of what is going on down
there in the bowels of Grosvenor Square.' I produced my
Number One Charming Smile. 'Because, to tell the truth,
for a mystery writer I hate real-life mysteries.'

'Nothing mysterious.' He brushed aside the idea as if
it had been a wisp of the Thames fog outside the windows. 'I don't intend, of course, to tell you the whole
story, but I can certainly point that imaginative mind of
yours in a direction.'

'That is my fondest wish.'

'I wonder,' he said after a moment, 'if you have any
idea how close to the edge of catastrophe Europe is.'

I picked up the cue at once, knowing Jean-Luc's
politics. 'The left gains power every day,' I suggested.
'The autumn elections can plunge France and Italy into
the Communist camp.'

His long, narrow head inclined sideways like a Balinese
dancer's, his high forehead white as bone in the flickering
firelight. 'You must know that, short of a coup d'état, the
forces of law and order are helpless to stem this tide. The
reds have taken the legal route, the parliamentary route,
the route of representative democracy. It was a black day
when they abandoned conspiracy and revolt.'

'And now it's too late for the forces of law and order to clamp down without looking like fascist swine,' I said in as polite a tone as possible.

He eyed me for a sign of sarcasm, but my face was as bland as I could make it under that basilisk stare of his. 'We have our ways,' he said in a dead voice.

'Don't waste time worrying,' he went on, 'that we'll let power slip from our hands. We have held it too long to let someone trick it away on the pretext of a mandate from the voters. But the times are such —' He stopped himself and made a pain-in-stomach gesture, as if his dinner was troubling him. 'Our first line of defence is not repression, it's the damned ballot boxes. We must play the same game the Reds do. So this autumn, we have to make sure the ballot boxes are filled with our own votes.'

'That would require a lot of men.'

'We have them.'

'And a lot of money. A war chest unheard of in size. Not millions of dollars. Tens of millions.'

Heavy lids hooded his glance for a moment. 'Such sums can be gathered. Those who support law and order can call on leaders all over the Western community of nations for substantial contributions.'

There was a queer silence in the air. I cleared my throat. 'In cash?' I asked.

He said nothing. A strange tingle went across my shoulder blades as if someone had run an ice cube over my bare skin.

Millions in cash. A war chest large enough to *buy* the autumn elections, to buy both the votes outright and the hoods that would keep opposition voters at home, to buy election judges, ballot tally's, fake demonstrations, 'leftist' outrages complete with false sets of political demands, gangs of tough youthful vandals masquerading as 'Maoist' thugs, phoney letter and telegram campaigns, sabotage to the opposition candidates, espionage and blackmail within their camp, the whole deadly toolkit by which elections had been burglarized for decades in the

134

States, and in Europe, too, for all I knew.

If it had been my strategy, I would have broken down the war chest and stashed it in various vaults around Europe. I yearned, I ached to ask the question I knew Dorani wouldn't answer. Why in God's name had he tucked all of it away in the vaults of the Manhattan Bank and Trust Company's branch on Grosvenor Square?

CHAPTER TWENTY-TWO

While it was not a pleasure doing business with Jean-Luc Dorani, it was better, as the saying goes, than a poke in the eye with a sharp stick. He had let me leave almost at once and had even offered to send me home in his car. I thanked him, but walked on Milmans Street to the Kings Road and picked up a taxi almost at once.

I had expected the feeling of supreme power one felt in the man. He was, after all, perhaps the single most powerful chieftain of crime in Europe. His connections were worldwide and lofty enough to allow him in and out of the US at will. His revenue was almost too large to estimate. And this would be just his illicit enterprises. I knew he was also heavily invested in legitimate business, like the rest of the fat cats.

What I got beyond a feeling of power was a very calm, almost deadly confidence. He had no doubts. The war chest he'd assembled would turn the tide. And if that didn't do it, the coup d'état would. It would not have been the first time gangsters were deputized to join police and soldiers in putting down popular uprisings. He could win. Total confidence.

More than confidence in himself, he seemed to have confidence in his connections, too. I wondered at what level he'd forged a link to Uncle. Fairly near the top?

Like poker players who never show you more of their hand than they need to beat the cards you hold, Dorani would probably know more about me than the Yugoslav escapade. But what he'd recalled for me was done with precision. His silence was worth, to me, what my nonintervention in the vault heist meant to him.

But why? Why was the man whose vaults were about to be looted so interested in keeping me from interfering with the robbery? None of it made sense, if one assumed, as I did, that all Dorani wanted to protect was his immense cache of election money. Or was he carrying, as well, a contract on Moe Gordon?

The cab was moving at a good clip along the Kings Road. We turned up Sloane Street into Knightsbridge and sped through Hyde Park Corner to Piccadilly. I began to rethink the whole situation, not from what Jean-Luc had given me, but from what I now saw he had had the strength and facilities to do.

He had, to begin with, replaced Dave with a *doppelgänger*. True, Dave's job in the bank was an isolated one. His co-workers rarely saw him. Replacing him was not easy, but not as difficult as it might have been. But the very act of replacing him suggested that Dave had been Moe Gordon's man and that Jean-Luc didn't trust him. In turn, this pointed to a split between the two mobmen. The war chest was Dorani's, but it undoubtedly contained money from the States.

Since Moe was out of favour with the twenty-six families, they would sooner kill him than trust him with their money. I had to cast Gordon in a new role. He wasn't part of the inner circle. He was operating outside. If he hadn't been allowed to join Jean-Luc's operation, perhaps he'd seen an opportunity to rip it off. And perhaps Dorani was carrying with him the families' contract to have Moe Gordon eliminated.

But why did it have to be a contract placed by the families? Another interest might have made the deal with Dorani. Perhaps it was this contract that came first in the tangled skein of events.

It was possible that I'd judged the priorities backwards. The cache of election money had perhaps been placed in London deliberately to attract Moe Gordon's interest.

If one retraced things from this starting point, with the

understanding that the original and primary goal was to eliminate Moe, then the cache of money was like the goat tethered in a jungle clearing for the stalking tiger to find. One didn't, after all, kill Moe Gordon casually. One had to have a reason. So, one engineered a reason.

And Moe had fallen for it. Like the rankest amateur.

Dorani's cunning was immense. For reasons known better to him than to me, he'd been quite sure Moe would go for the bait. To eliminate Moe, he had to trap him into committing a crime for which the only punishment was death.

From the beginning Dorani had counted on Moe's greed.

I sat there, not believing what I'd been thinking. The idea of one master hood ripping off another was not unheard of, especially if one of them were out of favour and slated for a hit. But to loot his own organization's European war chest of funds collected and earmarked for the autumn elections was a reckless act of defiance. Moe Gordon hadn't made his name by suicidal recklessness, but by safe, spider-like cunning.

He had to be a far more desperate man than most of us realized. Only Dorani had measured his greed with deadly accuracy.

My cab turned into St James's Street. Farther up the street, dark now after so many years of good eating, stood the old Prunier's restaurant corner. I was looking at it and, at the same time, thinking of getting to bed early and alone.

The combination was peaceful and reassuring to contemplate. So much so that when the taxi suddenly braked to a halt in front of where Prunier's had been – several blocks short of the driveway into Blue's, I at first was hardly aware that we had stopped.

I assumed traffic had halted us, yet there was no vehicle ahead. As this registered, the doors of the cab opened from both sides.

Two men got in. The lad with the short curly blond hair showed me something that could have been a water pistol but more closely resembled a Cobra five-shot special with a short barrel.

The other man sat beside me. Curly pulled down the jump seat and faced me, holding the gun out of sight between his thighs. His pose would have given the Freudians food for thought. As he had been assigned the gun, so, too, was he assigned the first line.

'Easy does it,' he said in a midwest US accent.

'From the song of the same name,' I added almost in an undertone.

'What-what?' the man to my left asked in a high quack.

I turned to him. He was older than either Curly or I, a seasoned hand, mid-forties, dark-grey lounge suit, pale-blue shirt, dark-blue tie, small knot. His big head and chin were seemingly cut off from the rest of him by the tightly secured shirt collar. He displayed milky blue eyes, a pug nose and a lovely row of capped teeth as he half snarled at me in a creditable imitation of a lion at bay. *I* was at bay, however, which tended to get motives mixed from the start. Why should he show fear?

'Smart bastard,' Blue-Eyes told me. 'But just not smart enough.'

His accent wasn't quite American. I judged he'd originally come from the States but had spent a long time in England. In that case he could well have been the local station agent in charge, except for two things: I was not big enough to warrant the top man and, in any case, I would have known his face if he ranked that high in Intelligence.

'My name is Patrick,' I said then, extending my right hand to him. 'Nice to meet a fellow American.'

He flinched, as if I'd drawn a gun from somewhere, then stared down at my hand like a man contemplating a tarantula. 'Let's skip the chit-chat,' he muttered through those beautiful caps. He leaned forward and tapped on the glass that separated us from the driver. 'Take off. Destination R.'

I turned to Curly. 'My name is Patrick,' I said, extending my right hand to him. 'Nice to meet a fellow American.'

He had the good sense to grin. 'We've met, Mr Patrick.'

'So we have. Almost a final meeting, wasn't it?' His face remained placid, his gun hand relaxed and steady. 'Better luck next time.' There was an uncomfortable pause. 'Or is this next time?' I asked then.

I had gone through several evaluations of Curly, based on past performance. That he was green, that he was accomplished, that he was stupid ... but I now decided that he was good, hard to rattle, terribly calm.

The other one was over the hill, sweating now, exuding the unmistakable odour of fear, that brass-and-sweat odour that tells you, against all appearances, that the man is afraid of you and not vice-versa. It made no sense for him to be afraid. He had all the cards. He had the troops.

And he had me.

CHAPTER TWENTY-THREE

It had never occurred to me before that doing business with the head of the Union Corse would be a picnic compared to dealing with agents of my own nation's security. At least, I assumed they were Uncle's. They handled routine in the normal Uncle way. If they weren't Uncle's, they once had been. That much I was sure of.

The cab made its way deep into Mayfair and, for a moment, I had the crazy idea that they were taking me to the Embassy. But the cab continued to Oxford Street and then rushed west, along Bayswater Road and the top of Hyde Park, until it reached Notting Hill Gate. We were, in fact, not too far from Jane Tait's flat.

The cab moved ahead more slowly now under the new leaves of a tree-lined street with wide front lawns, probing southward a bit into Holland Park. Finally the cab turned right into a driveway lined with high bushes. It whipped down an incline and turned sharp left into an underground garage. The doors shut behind us.

'Ah, yes,' I said. 'Destination R. Thank you driver.'

Curly smiled. I had made a big hit with him. It looked like he was about to make one on me.

That breathless sensation that one gets in these circumstances was now constricting the passage of air as it coursed up and down my throat. Or so it seems in these cases. A kind of knot forms below the adam's apple that one hesitates to relieve by swallowing, since this movement is such a well-known symptom of fear.

Fear was what I felt and didn't want to project. I'm not sure why a certified monster of crime like Dorani didn't inspire the kind of fear these two did. Perhaps it was because I'd been on their side of the transaction often enough to know the disregard of consequences one feels when carrying out government policy.

All law flows from government. So does lawlessness. Only government can label something a crime. It will not so label crimes of its agents – soldiers, the police, operatives like these men – and so it removes that crushing syndrome of consequences built into us by Judeo-Christian upbringing.

In such a vacuum, such an absence of morality, the focus of it – the animal in the trap, me – feels strangely isolated from the rest of humanity. Prisoners undergoing torture have that feeling. And, although they'd yet to lay a hand on me, I felt it now.

Curly didn't bother me as much as the man who was afraid of me. Curly just did his job, mindless when he had to be. Blue-Eyes was another matter. Something personal was at stake between us, something that had him sweating.

We were in the cellar of a large house now, having walked there along a concrete-lined tunnel from the underground garage. I passed rooms whose doors were open for ventilation and I caught a glimpse of the kind of monitoring equipment with which I'd once been so familiar.

We have these spy stations everywhere in Western Europe. That there was such an eavesdropping station in London wasn't surprising. There were probably a handful of them operated around the city by US personnel, and perhaps fifty more that the Brits and European nations were working. London isn't the largest centre of world espionage, but it's not an area to ignore when monitoring conversations.

That they had marched me past the evidence of such a station augered ill. They obviously didn't give a damn what I knew, including the location of this house. We ended in a largish room about twenty feet square with the standard plain wooden table in the centre, flanked by the uncomfortable wooden chairs and the painfully efficient floodlamps.

Question Time.

It may have been the lack of oxygen in the stale air. More likely it was my own emotional response that made it hard for me to breathe properly. I tried to control the scope of my breathing, to avoid giving away clues. But tempering the extremes of it only increased my need for oxygen.

They indicated one of the chairs and I sat down. They swivelled the lights to shine in my face, but didn't turn them on. Overhead a pale fluorescent ceiling fixture bathed all of us indifferently in a ghastly bluish glare.

Blue-Eyes stayed on his feet. Curly sat down and reached under his right arm, as if for a second gun. Instead he removed a mini-recorder and laid it on the table. Its cassette reels were already turning. The chit-chat in the cab had been recorded for posterity. So was what we would be saying next.

The standing man's odour was very noticeable now. I tried to think of his fear as a positive factor on my behalf. As a thought, it got nowhere. 'Let's start at the beginning,' he said then.

We waited. Was I supposed to say something? I cleared my throat. 'Go ahead,' I urged.

'Smart bastard,' Blue-Eyes muttered. He sucked in a great lungful of air through his gorgeous capped teeth. So he was having trouble with the air, too. 'Start talking.'

'Tell me what you want to know,' I said at last.

He shook his head from side to side, then forgot to stop. It kept shaking as he said: 'This will get just as hard as you make it. It's up to you.'

I shrugged. 'I didn't say I wouldn't talk. But you have to give me a clue. Talk about what?'

He bared his teeth again. 'Let's start with the fact that you're back in the business again.'

The accusation came out of left field, as far as I was

concerned. 'I'm still in the book-writing business, that's all.'

'We picked you up on Dorani's tail in New York,' he snapped back. 'Now we pick you up after conferring with Dorani in London.'

'Nice work.'

This got a smile out of Curly and a fiercer snarl out of the standing man. 'You admit it?' he pounced.

'I admit it.' I gestured with what I hoped was ease. 'I told you, I'm not a hostile witness. I'll talk.'

The older man paused for a moment. He'd obviously expected to produce more of a shock with his revelation. He started to say something else. Then his eyes crawled sideways, as if taking in the effect of all this on Curly. Slowly, he sat down on the other chair.

'Patrick,' he said then, 'I don't think you understand what a thin string you're hanging on.'

'About as thin as that cable on the elevator car in Atlanta.'

His milky eyes were almost invisible as he squinted hard at me, his beefy face turning a shade of magenta. 'Thinner,' he rasped. 'The only reason you're still alive is that you kept your nose out of the business. As long as you kept clear of us, we let the whole thing ride.'

I was beginning to understand his drift, or thought I did. I already knew I could use some of my information in books, as long as I changed names and places around. I could even travel freely, picking up background. But now I realized I couldn't poach on anything Uncle had going at the moment. Stupid of me not to have guessed. Uncle and Dorani were doing something together and I'd barged in on it.

Obviously, by so doing, I was jeopardizing the stand-off arrangement between Uncle and me. I did my best to look contrite and crestfallen at the same time.

'Hey,' I said softly. 'I had no idea—' I stopped and intensified my look of having been caught with my hand in the invisible cookie jar. 'I can see how it would look

144

to you,' I went on then. 'But, believe me, I'm out of the business. I don't have any interest in Dorani.'

'Then he has in you,' Blue-Eyes grunted.

'Let me tell you in all candour,' I began, inching closer to the recorder as it reeled endlessly on, 'that I'm into an exposé of the Unione Corse. Christ, everybody's writing about the Mafia. But I can scoop them all if I can bring out a book on Dorani and his boys. That's why we were talking. He found out what I was up to.'

'And called you in?' the older man hooted in disbelief. 'How come you left his house alive?'

I chuckled. 'What makes you think Dorani's averse to publicity?'

His state of disbelief looked very little different from his snarl of animosity. Whoever had capped those top teeth of his had done a magnificent job of protecting Blue-Eyes' dominant character traits. But I noticed that his face had resumed its calm, suety look. My story was getting to him.

'Don't kid me, Patrick.'

'The truth. He doesn't mind my doing the book. What he minds is not consulting with him first.'

'Bullshit.'

'I'm serious. So is he.' I warmed to my impromptu fiction now. 'Look at it from his viewpoint. Suppose he's got some bigwig on the hook for a large debt. The guy is slow in paying. Maybe he's toying with the idea of stiffing Dorani, or bargaining him down. He picks up my book, finds out what the Unione Corse is all about and, whoosh! His cheque's in the mail to Dorani the next morning.'

Curly liked the picture I had painted. He smiled again. His boss chewed on the idea for a long moment. 'Only one thing wrong with that story,' he said then. 'The Corsican code of silence is even stronger than the Mafia's *omertá*.'

'Which the Sicilians break every day.'

I had him there. He knew as well as I that these underworld codes of silence and honour and revenge were largely fictitious. When it suited a mobster to break the code, he broke it. And usually for big profits. Or, calculatedly, to misdirect the police.

Both men were quiet for a long moment now. The silence grew to several minutes in length. Then Blue-Eyes stirred. 'What's Dorani been feeding you?'

'Nothing specific.'

He chewed on this for a while, too. 'Like what?'

I gestured largely. 'Like their smuggling operations.'

'Ancient history.'

'Their ties with the international network.'

'Old hat.'

'Their investments in the resort industry.'

He eyed me sourly. 'What about their political work?'

I produced a puzzled frown. 'For what? Corsican independence?'

The older man was watching me closely now. 'Okay, what did he tell you about Corsican independence?'

'They're against it.'

'What else?'

'Nothing else. I got the feeling politics has a low priority with them.'

'What else?'

'That's about it.'

'What else?' he demanded.

I gestured hopelessly. He sat back, trying to hide a look of satisfaction. Since Curly's face had given away nothing during all this, he had no trouble hiding whatever feelings he had about my testimony, or lack of it.

But Blue-Eyes' question had given me a compass bearing. Uncle was concerned about Dorani's political work. And, from what Dorani had told me, his work was all in support of the right-wing segment of the Establishment. Surely that had to be where Uncle's sympathies also lay?

Was that why this man was afraid? Did he think I might have uncovered some clandestine deal between Dorani and Uncle? But if I had, what could I do with the information? Who'd buy it? Or was he afraid I'd use it, thinly disguised, in a novel?

I hoped I'd been convincing when I denied any knowledge of Dorani's political moves. I had a feeling my life depended on not knowing. Especially not knowing about the war chest in the Manhattan Bank's vault on Grosvenor Square.

The older man sighed hungrily and bared his teeth yet again, as if filtering some sort of impurities out of the air. Then he let a satisfied look show as he turned to Curly. 'You got all that?'

Curly ducked his chin in a sure-enough gesture. He put the Cobra down on the table to pick up the mini-recorder, switch it off, roll the tape back a few inches and play it.

'. . . else?' Blue-Eyes' voice demanded.

'That's about it,' my own voice echoed with a tinny distortion.

Without even trying, I could have grabbed the revolver. Was it some kind of test? Would I find it empty of bullets? But I could see the cylinder from where I sat, and the hollow-nosed dumdum slugs were clearly visible. Perhaps the firing pin had been removed?

Or else I'd once again overestimated Curly. Maybe he was as hopeless an amateur as he had seemed originally. In fact, I asked myself now – feeling the itch in my fingers to snatch up the gun but resisting it – wasn't this whole operation inept? They'd picked up my connection with Dorani but not with Rosalind Rue and her protector.

Or were they simply remaining mute on that point, for the time being?

I couldn't stand it. I grabbed the Cobra.

The older man's teeth showed as he hissed like a cat. Curly's face froze.

I flipped the gate open and examined the cartridges. Then I pulled back the hammer and saw the perfectly good firing pin. Finally, I closed the gate and, holding the gun by its stubby barrel, handed it back to Curly.

'Can I go now?' I asked.

CHAPTER TWENTY-FOUR

I am not known for common sense. If I'd stopped to ponder my move, I would have ruled out the whole grandstand play with the gun.

But as it turned out Curly's laugh when I handed him the gun seemed to break up the tension irretrievably. Blue-Eyes hated me even more and he hadn't for a moment lost his fear. But in the face of his colleague's laughter, he had to revert to Mister Reasonable.

Evidently, too, he was satisfied that I knew nothing of Dorani's political involvement. Most probably it was a top secret project that Blue-Eyes himself was managing for Uncle. He seemed to be in charge of the whole shooting match, which helped account for all that sweat.

At that moment I was, without being aware of it, in the classic 'had I but known' position of the spunky heroine of a woman's gothic novel. Had I but known, indeed. Had I but known why Blue-Eyes was so sweaty I'd have dropped a few pints myself.

As it was, I was just stupid enough to convince them that I was very stupid. They seemed almost glad to get rid of me.

They sent me home in the same cab they'd hijacked. And Uncle even let me pay the fare myself, detour mileage and all.

'You're all heart,' I told the driver.

'Listen, I have to answer to my dispatcher for what's on the meter.'

'You could've shut it off while I was in the cellar.'

He got me to Blue's in a hurry and didn't complain when I failed to tip him. I stood for a moment in the turnabout area of cobblestones, breathing the good damp night air of London and feeling lucky about the whole encounter.

Lucky and puzzled. I no longer had doubts about Curly being inept, or that Uncle paid his salary. Only one thing puzzled me now: how a nation considered a Superpower could waste so much tax money on so little in the way of effective service. The taxpayers were being had.

I'd been out of that service almost six years now, long enough for the faces to be new. Evidently the minds behind the faces were different, too. Apparently Intelligence work, which had once seemed a lonely and dangerous thing – bulwarked by one's own idealistic motives, however mistaken – had changed. It was just another government job now.

Curly's view of himself and of his work seemed typical of the new breed, civil servants indistinguishable in many ways from postmen or garbage collectors or statisticians or school teachers. The perks of the job – tenure, health insurance, retirement benefits, regular merit increases – had become more important than the job itself.

It wasn't that people like Curly were lazy. They were simply new people with a new way of looking at Intelligence work. It was more important to this new breed of agent that his personnel reports be seamlessly uneventful than that he made sure a suspect didn't get a chance at his gun.

I smiled, realizing that Curly would make a better agent than I'd once been. He wouldn't become disillusioned, as I had. He had no illusions to begin with. In the long run, he was better for Uncle than I'd ever been.

He certainly was better from my viewpoint, too. If he'd been doing his work twenty-four hours a day he'd have spotted the Rosalind Rue connection. His superior, the meathead with the blue eyes and the body odour, was obviously assigned only to keep an eye on Dorani's political manoeuvring. That was as far as his brief carried him.

The fact that Rosalind Rue's protector might be planning to upset the operation hadn't yet intruded itself into his management of the case. When it did, my life wasn't going to be worth anything to either of the two men who had carelessly let me go tonight. Once they connected Moe Gordon to me, and both of us to Dorani's vault in the Manhattan Bank, they would snuff me without hesitation.

I had no written standoff agreement with Uncle. He interpreted its terms as he saw fit. I realized now how close he was to foreclosing me. In the interests of self-preservation, it was time to take Jean-Luc's advice and get the hell out of the caper.

That much money was tempting. From the beginning, the smell of it had lured me steadily onward. But not towards self-destruction. I hadn't bargained for that. Dorani and the men Uncle had set to watching him would see to my destruction if I kept swimming in their stream.

It was time to get out, dry off and go home. In one piece.

I went inside the hotel, retrieved the envelope I'd left for Jane Tait and made it upstairs to my room.

The moment I opened my door and reached for the wall switch the room exploded with light. In the corridor behind me a disembodied voice muttered: 'Straight ahead' before prodding something hard in the small of my back. I went straight ahead.

'This the monkey?' Moe Gordon asked the young man with the olive eyes.

He rubbed his chin where my knee had caught his trigeminal nerve. 'Yeh.' The man behind me jabbed his gun even harder into my back.

'Inside. Close the door. Sit down.' Moe Gordon had one of those soft, hoarse voices that seemed to have been used in all sorts of weather and left out to dry with rust spots on it.

He had a pleasant, tanned face, thin and not terribly lined by his nearly seventy years. His big, fawn's eyes under bushy eyebrows were a dove-grey colour, like the coat an undertaker wears for morning funerals.

He sat absolutely at ease on my sofa, one leg over the other, one arm over the other, crossed at the wrist as Jack Benny did it. He had a soft, almost uninterested gaze that made no attempt at drilling a glance into my soul, Dorani style. Perhaps he knew better.

'Sonny,' Moe Gordon told me as I sat down across from him, 'I got one sore boychick here.' He indicated his soft-chinned employee. 'He is dying to even up with you for that job you done on him. Right Angie?'

Angie made a face. 'When I get t'rough wit' you shit-head, the skin will be hangin' off you in strips a yard long. You gonna *beg* me to kill you.'

I nodded, remembering an ancient wisdom of Dashiell Hammett's: the cheaper the crook, the gaudier the patter. I wished for Hammett to be here. I yawned, not because I was bored, but because fear was again depriving me of the use of oxygen.

'Where is the girlie?' Moe Gordon asked politely, with about the same emotion as if he'd asked how the weather was outside.

'Why don't you have Angie work me over first?' I suggested.

'Not a bad idea. And Nico here can help him.'

'A sure way not to find her.'

'I don't know,' Moe Gordon said in a philosophic tone. 'We got all night. These two *bulvans* and me, we got till nine-thirty a.m. to get answers.'

I yawned again; the tension was making me almost high with breathlessness. Nine-thirty was the hour the US Embassy vault would open and Gordon expected his sappers to walk out past Clarissa carrying the proceeds of the vault heist.

We had ten hours, during which Angie or Nico could certainly get me to talk. I am no better than the next person at standing up to pain. Cuddly Grandpa was giving me time to sort it all out, I could see that. He felt confident I would tell him what he wanted to know.

'Where were you shipping her in that trunk?' I asked. 'She could have smothered.'

'Not possible,' Gordon assured me in his rachitic voice. 'I love that little girlie. I want only the best for her. And that's what she's getting, sonny. The very best.'

'Funny way to give it to her. This moron had her strangled with that gag.' I nodded at Angie. 'You send a goon on an errand of mercy? I thought you had judgement, Moe.'

'Moe he calls me.' Gordon said to some imaginary audience. 'Meets me two minutes ago and already it's first names.'

'If that offends you, imagine how you'd feel when she arrived dead because this *djibrone* tied off her windpipe. He's a killer, not a nursemaid.'

For an instant I saw Moe Gordon's big soft eyes flick in Angie's direction. But he had disciplined himself too well to rise to the crude bait I was dangling. He wasn't about to let me start an argument between him and one of his underlings. Still, I thought I had done Angie's reputation a bit of damage. Maybe more than that.

'You gonna listen to a shithead?' Angie burst out in a sore voice. He was a third Moe Gordon's age, and too stupid not to take my bait. 'The first thing I cut off is that lying tongue of his.' He whipped out one of those fat-handled Swiss Army knives and flipped open its main blade.

'Easy, Angie,' his boss said.

But Angie wasn't taking lessons tonight. 'First he Japs me fighting dirty. I was lying like a lox on them bricks. Then he tells lies about me. And I'm supposed to take it easy?'

'You're surrounded by low-end material, Moe,' I told him in a pleasant, conversational tone, as devoid of emotion as his own. 'Having this creep on your payroll is like having lice.'

'He walks in here,' Gordon told the room at large, 'about half an inch away from being a stiff, and already he's giving advice.'

Nico, the stocky man who had propelled me forward into the room, shifted his blue-steel Colt .45 automatic from his right hand to his left in order to scratch his broken nose. 'Maybe,' he said then in a slow, thoughtful voice, as if supplying a missing entry in a crossword puzzle, 'he don't believe he's a goner.'

Moe Gordon inclined his head in the direction of the sage remark, but his big Bambi eyes stayed on me. 'You hear, sonny?' he asked me. 'Even a punchy palooka like Nico's got it straight. I don't claim my fellas are geniuses.' A modest smile pursed his lips. 'For more than one genius this world don't got no room.' The smile faded abruptly. 'But they know what happens to you if you don't give me the girlie.'

'Sad.' I let the silence gather.

After a moment Moe Gordon shifted on the sofa. 'Sad?'

'Sad.'

More silence. 'What sad?' he demanded at last.

'Sad to see a man with your brains on the level of these *brutti animali*.' I went so far as to point my finger at Moe Gordon. What did I have to lose? 'You're letting cheap punks do your thinking. You, The Genius. If you ever stop to wonder some time what brought you so far down, Moe, take a look around at the reject crap you're using for helpers.'

A faint flare of irritation showed in his doe-eyes, but disappeared almost at once. He knew my game: not to stir him up, but to send the animals out of control, if I could. I decided to shift pressure slightly.

When one feels as much fear as I had been feeling to-night there is a plateau beyond which it isn't possible to feel more. Soldiers in combat know it. The body takes only so much, then it adapts to the symptoms. At that moment, on a relative basis, one becomes fearless, while still steeped in the stuff. What Uncle's two agents had started tonight, Gordon's boys were finishing. I was in a state of fear overload.

'When you surround yourself with this shit,' I went on, gathering together the scraps of a new idea, 'you're begging for it, Moe. What makes you think Dorani doesn't own these two grifters? Where is it written – on what tablet of stone? – that because they're stupid, vicious and corrupt, Dorani still might not be interested in buying them?'

I'd finally done something to the brain behind those kewpie-doll eyes under their arches of bushy eyebrows. If I wanted to consolidate the effect, I had to keep moving right along.

'You think it was just clumsiness that made Angie strangle the girl? She would've been DOA, Moe, a present to you from Dorani. And let me ask you something else. Why did Angie have to strip her naked to do the job?'

End of the fight. Moe Gordon's big eyes turned icy tan, like a coffee-flavoured popsicle. Still watching me closely, he said to the empty air around him. 'Nico, give me your piece. You and Angie take a walk. Hang around downstairs in the bar. I'll call if I need you.'

'Lis-sen,' Angie hissed. 'This *stronzo* is my meat.'

'I know,' Moe assured him. 'Nico, the piece.'

Nico handed the Colt automatic to Moe. The two men left the room. I sat there watching what had to be the prize collector's item of rarities, Moe Gordon with a gun in his hand. He probably hadn't held one since the 1920s when he got out of the contract murder business and into the money business.

'I don't believe what I'm seeing,' I said then.

He frowned slightly, more a contraction of eye muscles, as if reading an oculist's chart. 'Tell me, sonny, what gives you the *fegato* to jump salty with a fella old enough to be your father? You think I forgot which end is which on this thing?' He hefted the heavy automatic.

'An hour ago,' I said then, 'I was sitting across from

another man in your line of work. He's a high-strung type, fierce eyes, quick decisions. Total air of confidence. Am I telling you anything you don't know about Dorani?'

I took in a breath. The terrible emptiness in my lungs had gone away with the departure of the two thugs, either of whom might shoot first and figure it out later. Foxy Grandpa would work it the other way, or so I hoped.

'Now I'm sitting across from a man with twice Dorani's brains. Twice his experience. Ten times his balls. But am I looking at confidence? What I see is a man, for all his clout, on the run. Worse than that, a man who's given up a hostage to destiny.'

The tight look around his eyes deepened. 'What kinda crap talk is that? What destiny? What hostage? Talk American.'

'Without the girl, you'd be a free man. She's a millstone around your neck. Alone you'd be back on top in no time.'

It was just talk, wild words I was grinding out, trial balloons I hoped might tell me something. He seemed to slump on the sofa. The Colt, held alertly up, muzzle zeroed in on my stomach, drooped to one side and came to rest on his thigh. By God, I'd hit a nerve.

'The girlie,' he said, more to himself than to me. 'I love that girlie. Do I ever wonder what brought me down? Do you think —?' He hunched forward as if launching into a full confession.

'Do you for one second think I would be here if it wasn't for her? I didn't have to blow the States. There was no way they could tie me in.' His big eyes looked moist. 'Except for that little girlie. Do you think I didn't get the same advice a thousand times? "Moey, hit the broad," "Moey, waste the chick." But something's happened to The Genius, sonny. Here.' He touched his chest gently in the vicinity of where his heart might be. 'Her life,' he groaned, 'is that precious to me.'

'Your head's in the noose for love?' I asked. 'You're asking me to believe y —?'

'A man gets to a certain age. Christ, I had broads all my life, top ones. I swam in cunt, let me tell you. But this little girlie is something else. It's a matter of investment. I invested the tail end of my life in her. It's a commitment.'

I sat there unable to say anything in the face of this amazing admission. Rosalind Rue was a lovely woman. I had very little idea what she was really like, but the surface was superior.

I also knew Moe Gordon had done a lot for her over the years, not so much for her career, but for the same reason we all do things, for our own comfort and convenience. He liked her on hand. He kept her on hand. And now he was telling me she owned so much of his heart that he had —

Was that the reason Moe Gordon had thrown caution away and made a play for the Dorani war chest? Was he planning to disappear with his little girlie – plastic surgery for two, please – and live out his few remaining years on the millions he would take from the Manhattan Bank's vault?

It wasn't that bad an idea if he'd been a younger man. Even so, how could he keep Dorani's people from finding him? There is nothing like unlimited wealth in cash to let a man enjoy anonymity ... but against Dorani?

'Where could you hide that they wouldn't find you?'

His small body seemed to tighten into attention. He'd had no warning that I could see that far ahead in his plans. 'Explain yourself, sonny,' he demanded in a suddenly grim voice.

'Or you'll shoot me?' I added. 'That Colt doesn't give you leverage. Pull the trigger and you'll never see Rozzie again. Guaranteed.'

'What did Dorani tell you?' he asked.

'He didn't want anything big from me, like the whereabouts of a girl. So he didn't give anything big away.'

'Meaning?'

'You're asking for something important. So my price has to be important, too.'

'That makes you just another punk kidnapper.' He managed to get a certain tone of injured faith in his voice.

I shook my head. 'I'm a hi-jacker, Moe. And I hi-jacked more than a kidnapping.'

'So what's the ransom?'

'Half of what you find in the Manhattan Bank's vault.'

CHAPTER TWENTY-FIVE

Money talks. By midnight I'd adjusted the balance between Moe Gordon and me.

For one thing, he'd paid off Angie and sent him home. He kept the ex-pug Nico, however, and curiously enough he kept Nico's Colt .45, hanging loosely in the outside pocket of his jacket. Nico had borrowed a small fat belly-gun from Angie. Nobody was giving me close-up looks but it seemed to be a 'ladies' Beretta, .25 calibre.

I'll say this for the old-timer. He never let me get within a country mile of the Colt. He was old, but not senile. I would never have the chance at his gun that I had with the Cobra Curly had carelessly set down in front of me.

All my good intentions about getting out of the caper had now gone down the drain. Even if I'd wanted to obey Dorani's suggestion, even if I'd hoped to avoid stirring up Uncle, I was now sealed into the deal ... and at gunpoint, too.

I suppose I'll never know whether Moe Gordon was simply jollying me along until he would wipe me out, or really felt I was important enough to his plans to deal with me. I certainly worked hard convincing him that I knew his whole plan and how Dorani had already out-manoeuvred him.

Yes, I had a plan, too. We all had plans. I explained mine slowly and painstakingly to Moe. The Genius's mind was not what it had once been. He took information in very slow, reluctant sips.

Was it the effect of seeing his life iris down to a pinhole because of a woman? But who had invested her with the power to ruin him? Perhaps that knowledge alone had been enough to destroy Moe Gordon's self-confidence, his awareness that he had created his own doom.

As the hours passed and we refined my plan, Moe referred to the dark-haired woman many times, but I was unable to get him to expand on the secret he shared with her, the reason being her protector had forced him to leave the States.

'Why ship her somewhere in a trunk, for God's sake?' I asked at one point.

We had moved from my room to his sumptuous suite and were slowly sipping iced soda water as we reviewed what was left of our lives. Nico was asleep on a sofa, the Beretta in his right hand. I longed for sleep, too. Moe's Colt made a bulky bulge in his jacket pocket.

'Because she was never gonna go away with me on her own,' he responded.

Somewhere in the distance of London, fast asleep against a Monday rising, church bells tolled the hour of two a.m. In seven and a half hours the time-release locks on both vaults would click open within seconds of each other. In seven and a half hours perhaps the heist would stand or fall on what we planned here now.

I watched Moe's small, leathery face, his huge eyes dropping with fatigue. If he'd explained nothing else, he'd at least told me why he'd chosen that bizarre way to move Roz out of the country.

Obviously, if she were told she was slated for plastic surgery, an ID change and ten years of living death in some faraway village as the companion of a dying mobster, Roz would have balked. So she had to be drugged and crated.

Moe was being cruel only to be kind, if one's idea of kindness is exile, during which a gorgeous woman of thirty-three becomes a woman of forty-three with features changed by surgery and age. Like the rest of his planning,

Moe's scenario for the remainder of Rosalind Rue's youth and beauty was poorly conceived. The man whose mind had woven such beautiful arabesques of tax quasi-legalities, such intricate traceries of off-shore trusts and Swiss *stiftungs*, had sadly deteriorated.

'Kidnapping Rozzie was dumb,' I told him, too tired to mind my tongue. 'But at least, by brute force, it might have worked ... and made her hate you for the rest of your life. But the business with the vault!'

He looked pained and glanced at Nico to see if any of this constructive criticism was being overheard. Satisfied his flunky was asleep, he said: 'Just because Dorani tumbled to it? What does that prove?'

'That it was not a good plan,' I said as gently as possible. 'It started off smart but it turned dumb. Throwing a loop around Dave Greeley and his girlfriend in the Embassy next door was good. A little money bought the combo and gave you access to both ends of the operation. You put a sapper in the Embassy vault on Friday afternoon, right? Clarissa locked him in. She was supposed to let him out Monday morning with the loot from the bank vault.'

'All of which could still happen.'

'No. The way you set it up guaranteed its failure.'

I sipped cold soda water and wished for a taste to it. 'Your plan was too easy to hi-jack. What Dorani did was to replace the real Dave Greeley with a double. He had the real Greeley on ice and threatened Clarissa with killing her boyfriend. That kept her in line, not for your plan, but for Dorani's. Follow me?'

'Only too close, sonny.'

I nodded. 'Your plan tied up both ends of the heist. Dorani simply took it over. Now he controls both ends.'

A sound something like a muffled groan escaped the small, elderly mobster. It was not possible to like him. He was not a nice man. But cornered now, drained of confidence and clout, he was at least pitiable.

'The way I figure it,' I went on mercilessly, 'when the time-release mechanism lets go at nine-thirty a.m., Dorani's told Clarissa to re-lock the door manually. So your sapper can't escape that way. And the bogus Dave Greeley in the bank vault won't let him leave the other way with his —'

I grinned at him. It had just crossed my mind that I didn't know the size of the heist, either in money or in weight. 'What are we talking about?' I asked then. 'One bundle? How big?'

He took a long time answering. For a while it seemed that even with all the constructive advice I'd been giving him, he still didn't trust me worth a damn. On the other hand, I had disclosed Dorani's hand. It was worth something.

'Two Air France flight bags,' he said then. 'Those light blue jobs? Shoulder straps.'

I thought for a while. The largest convenient piece of paper currency, even though it's twice the size of a dollar, is the thousand-franc note printed by the Swiss. If the European political slush fund was stored that way, one could probably stack a single row of such notes to the height of about fourteen inches. With appropriate ties now and then of rubber or paper bands, one could probably load a flight bag with, say, a thousand of the valuable slips of paper currency, before the weight got too heavy for the vinyl shoulder strap.

That was over a million in Swiss francs. Per bag. Together, at current conversion rates, they contained almost a million US dollars in cash.

It didn't seem enough. Perhaps I'd underestimated how much could be stacked in two flight bags and conveniently carried by one man. Even if I had, the amount in those bags was still no more than two million dollars. I begun to see that, without once admitting what he was doing, Jean-Luc Dorani had misled me. I'd assumed his was *the* war chest, that there were no others. But obviously he had co-leaders in other parts of Europe who would have amassed their own slush funds, too, for the coming elections.

'Doesn't seem like much,' I told Moe Gordon then. 'Hardly worth either of us making a play for it this morning.'

'Shit it ain't.' He stared at me. Behind his fawn eyes something was stirring. Should I tell him, he seemed to be thinking. As if to reassure himself, he reached into his right-hand pocket and removed the Colt. He tucked it into his belt over the left hip and buttoned his jacket to hide it. But he remained silent.

'In other words,' I said, allowing a little sheer greed to show, 'my half could run as high as a million bucks.'

'Only if you earn it, sonny,' the mobster snapped with quite a show of alacrity for a geriatric gent long past his bedtime.

'I already have, tipping you off to Dorani. But there's a way to outwit him. I'll throw it in the pot.'

'Do that,' he urged.

'First you have to understand that going in and out of an embassy is a different matter from going in and out of a bank. There are guards in both places, but they're watching for different things. The Embassy guard tries to spot troublemakers, extremists. He's not looking to foil a heist but an incident, a protest or something. A man walking around an embassy with two Air France flight bags is not going to excite suspicion, especially if he's on his way out. He's just a visiting tourist, that's all.

'But a bank guard is a different proposition,' I went on. 'You can't suddenly show up at nine-thirty a.m., on your way upstairs from the bank's vault with two bags on your shoulder. He didn't see you come in. He's never seen those bags before. You'd never make it to the door before being stopped and searched.'

'Never mind the kindergarten lectures,' Moe Gordon said.

'If you insist. But it's already crossed your mind that

once Dorani got to that Clarissa girl, your sapper couldn't get out by way of the Embassy. He has to go through the bank because the Embassy vault door's still locked. That puts him directly in the hands of the bogus Dave Greeley. If he eludes him – why should he, since he thinks Dave's on your payroll? – then the lobby guard will stop him.'

'*Marrone.*'

'You see how Dorani's out-thought you?'

'Move along, sonny. No more lectures.'

'Okay. We need two empty Air France flight bags before nine-thirty a.m. Nico and I show up at the bank with the bags. We walk in. The guard sees the bags, which is what we want him to do. Now the two of us go down the stairs and the fake Dave lets me in through the glass door.'

'Why should he?'

'Because at three-thirty p.m. last Friday he told me to come back Monday morning. The bastard will remember. I'm counting on it.'

'Good. Continue.'

'Nico comes in with me and we put the fake Dave out of commission. There are little rooms down there where rich old ladies clip their coupons. The doors have locks. We can lock the fake Dave in one of those rooms.'

'Better. Continue.'

I smiled at him. He'd suddenly stopped looking so lost-lamb. It was the mention of the two empty flight bags that had done it. 'Now Nico goes halfway up the stairs to make sure nobody comes down and spoils everything. I go into the vault. I get rid of the empty flight bags. I pick up the full ones from your sapper.'

'Keep going, sonny.'

'I leave the vault, pick up Nico, breeze through the bank lobby under the nose of the guard and grab a cab outside.'

'To where?'

'Here? Wherever you say.'

'And Nico's there with you to make sure I get those flight bags,' Moe Gordon mused. 'Not a bad plan. Could you kind of weave one more thing into it.'

'What?'

'My little girlie.' His voice had gone down an octave. 'You don't think you're sitting here sipping soda, safe and sound, with Angie out of your hair and Nico fast asleep, because I really trust you? No, sonny, it's because you have Rozzie somewhere. That's your case ace. Now play it.'

I shrugged. 'If that's what you want.'

'You gotta be *meshuggah* not to know how much that girlie means to me.'

There was something in his voice that reverberated in the posh hotel suite like the knell of a great doomsday bell. I know I was being susceptible, taking him at his word. Yet I'd seen the passion that he was carrying. It was ... um ... operatic.

He really was Sicilian after all. This doomed love for a girl young enough to be his daughter? Hadn't he moulded her life for her as if she'd been a daughter? But a daughter whose sexual charms he had designed to entangle him hopelessly in some predestined horror neither one of us could guess at.

Why? He wasn't a teenager bursting with hormones. Or had it all been a blunder, one of those once-in-a-lifetime mistakes by which we continue to destroy ourselves in our own madness?

And, if so, what had the blunder been? Something hidden, but big. So big it had never been fully covered up but, like a water-bloated corpse, was rising to the surface once again, puffed with the foetid gasses of its own corruption.

'Which is why,' I said at last, 'you don't get the girl till this whole thing's over and done with. After I get my half, you get Rozzie.'

His face had darkened as he sat there thinking. Now

he began to shake his head from side to side. 'There's a hitch.'

'What?'

'A big hitch. How you gonna get my digger in the vault to give you the bags? He knows from nothing of all this. He's been locked in there since Friday evening with food and water and two oxygen tanks and a chemical toilet, even. It took us weeks to smuggle in all the crap through the Embassy.' He thought for a moment. 'His name's Harry Finch. A Limey specialist. Use his name.'

'Can I use your name with him?'

He nodded. 'Maybe you can talk him into it. You're a born con-man anyway.'

Knowing the sapper's name helped, but it would take more than talk to disarm his caution. 'Has he ever seen Dave Greeley?'

Moe frowned. 'No. But he knows the name. He didn't have to know what Greeley looked like because he was going out the Embassy route. All I told him was Greeley was our man who had switched off the sound sensor alarm.'

'So I'm Dave Greeley. That'll help.'

For the first time in several hours, Moe Gordon smiled.

Confidential Internal report, Criminal Intelligence Division, US Department of Justice, 2 July:

We now assign an unofficial and approximate dollar weighting of $7.4 billion as the annual revenue of those legal and/or illegal activities within the 50 states which are owned and/or operated by enrolled and/or affiliated members of the families of organized crime. This places the so-called National Crime Syndicate and/or Organized Crime in a position secondary only to General Motors, but with an estimated 53.7 per cent in cash flow, the bulk of it untaxed and/or unreported.

CHAPTER TWENTY-SIX

All along I have been giving you tidbit insights into crime, I hope, a sort of 'Introduction to Law-Breaking 201'. Let me add a thought based on Moe's characterization of me: no one cons better than a con-man.

Perhaps the whole mystique of trying to merchandise plausibility does something to the wariness of the person creating the deception. In putting together his con, the con-man asks himself at each stage: 'is this believable?' and in this way he begins to deceive himself by giving himself the benefit of the doubt. 'Will the sucker buy the con?' he asks himself. The answer is usually 'of course he will'. In that way a new sucker is born: himself.

Whatever the reasons – and Moe Gordon was less a con-man than an employer of con-men, as well as murderers – he bought my con. Or seemed to.

He woke the slumbering Nico and briefed him fully. He even allowed me to leave Blue's Hotel – this was five in the morning – with full confidence that I would come back to him from a sleeping city with two Air France flight bags.

Not easy. I left Blue's on foot and walked up St James's to Jermyn Street, turned right and moved along quickly in the darkness. Nobody seemed to be following me, certainly not Curly in his Austin Mini. The sky would lighten soon enough, too soon for me. Past Fortnum's I hiked, tired but keyed up beyond any excitement I'd felt before. Behind the National Westminster Branch in Piccadilly I stepped inside one of the red telephone booths and called Jack Philemon. He didn't waken easily. On the tenth bzz-bzz he picked up the phone.

'Max?'

'Jack, how fast can you meet me near New Bond Street?'

'Wh—? Y'mean naow?' he asked, drawling it out like a sulky child.

'I mean ten minutes.'

'Jaysus H. Kuh-royst.'

'I'll need you till ten this morning, Jack. That's five hours' work.'

'Throw in breakfast, sweetums?'

'How about, um, a thousand an hour?'

'Pounds,' he snapped quickly.

'Pounds,' I agreed. 'The back of Air France, via Bruton Street to Barlow Place. Look for me.'

'Ten minutes.' The line went dead.

He was there in nine minutes. In the half-dark his peculiar redhead's complexion looked muddy with sleep, the freckles like dark moles or liver spots. 'Wot ho, Max, me boy?'

We stood at the rear of the four-storey Air France building in a kind of slanting alley-way. A large, prominent AFA burglar alarm had been installed over one of the rear doors. Jack eyed it apprehensively.

The building's fourth floor was set back slightly, a kind of penthouse with many windows. But starting at the third floor two very sturdy drainpipes descended. The joints in the pipes were staggered, almost as if the workmen who had installed them had arranged for a climber to have a foothold every few feet on his upward journey.

Jack went first and I followed. We found it no harder than if the architect had thoroughly provided ladders for our convenience. So much for burglary precautions. If Air France reads this now, *mefiez-vous, mes amis.*

I didn't need to explain to a professional like Jack Philemon that with the exception of banks – and even with some banks – the weakest 'wall' of any building is its roof. Get on to it and all doors are as gauze through which one can flit with the ease of, um, ectoplasm. Another lecture topic for 'Introduction to Law-Breaking 201'.

We got through a window in the four-storey office. Moving quietly down the inner stairs to the ground floor, we conferred in front of the door to the ticket office. 'No night man,' I murmured.

'Alarm system can't pick us up going out, either.'

I didn't know the routine in London but in New York the valuable item in a ticket office is the validator plate that the reservationist slips into his or her stamping machine.

One stamp of a validator plate makes an expensive airline ticket out of a bit of printed booklet. In the States, organized crime steals ticket stock from one place, validator plates from another, and begins selling trips to faraway places at half off the list price.

Law-abiding Americans, who'd never buy stolen goods, grab these discount tickets because they come with some sort of conscience-assuaging story of a friend who had to give up his ticket at the last moment and will take half what he paid. Nobody believes the story, but one needs something to hang on to in this cynical world, doesn't one?

I'd guess that Air France's validator plates were as much a target for thieves in London as New York. But the airline didn't need an expensive perimeter alarm system to protect something the size of a matchbook. The plates would be tucked away in a wall safe with its own alarm.

We could, in other words, loid our way through the inner back door of the ticket office without too much fear of setting off an alarm. Or so Jack and I decided in a quick interchange of grunts and whispers.

But a loid didn't do it. An additional edge of steel had been welded to the doorframe, covering the slit through which celluloid could normally be inserted. Jack shook his head. We were working by the glow of a penlight. He reached in his pocket and brought out what looked like a large marker pen.

'Get a load of this,' he muttered.

Under the rays of the penlight I saw what it was, a screwdriver with an unusually broad head. Then Jack unscrewed the end of it and I saw that nestled inside were a whole set of tubes that twisted into each other, making a lever over a metre long. From a screwdriver, the thing had grown into a pry-bar, or what the English burglar calls a jemmy.

A minute later the door frame buckled just enough to one side under this leverage to let the door swing open. We fanned out in two directions through the darkened ticket office. It was Jack who finally found the cache of bags in a closet of a side room marked 'Sales'.

We took two, climbed up the inside stairs and out on to the roof. It was now almost six a.m. The sky was light in the east. In three and a half hours the time-release locks on both vault doors would open.

We shinned down the drainpipes even more readily than we'd climbed them, and moved quickly out of the area. A coffee place on Albermarle Street, down the block from Brown's Hotel, was just opening for the early trade.

We sat at a table, sipping hot coffee. Jack gave me a funny look as I tucked the light blue flight bags under my chair. 'Some new sort of fetish, old man?' he inquired politely. 'I've heard of having a thing about rubber. It's vinyl now, is it?'

'Jack, this is where you memorize the next step.'

'Ah, a *next* step. Fully logical as this one, I dare say?'

I grinned at him. 'You have two more jobs this morning. They'll take you from nine-thirty to ten-thirty a.m. That's only one more hour of work and I'm paying the waiting time between now and then.'

'Ta, guv.' He pulled his forelock reverently.

I noticed an evening newspaper from the day before

that someone had left on the table. I opened the two flight bags and carefully stuffed them with newspaper to make them look full. Jack nodded appreciatively, as if he knew what I had in mind. He didn't, but I soon set that straight.

I told him then what he had to do between nine-thirty and ten-thirty to earn his money. And mine.

CHAPTER TWENTY-SEVEN

The rest of it was easy. Well, the first half of it, anyway.

In my own planning – which I didn't share with Moe Gordon – I had divided the morning's work into two phases. The first part went pretty well, if I do say so myself.

At nine-twenty, Nico, the small black .25 calibre Beretta, and I were in an ordinary taxi crusing along Piccadilly. We had given the driver three destinations, a fake one near the bank in order to time our arrival accurately, the Manhattan Bank itself and a quick return to Blue's Hotel.

The fake call was at my publisher's, which we reached at nine-twenty-six. I went up to the door, knocked, got no answer and quickly returned to the cab. 'Not open yet. On to the bank,' I directed. It was nine-twenty-nine as Nico and I got out of the taxi. My mouth was dry. I was breathing fast.

'We shouldn't be more than five minutes, if that,' I told the driver.

'Good-o,' he said.

We had a short flight of very broad limestone steps to climb. By the time we reached the entrance I was out of breath. The guard inside stooped with keys in hand behind the glass door to open the locks at the top and bottom. He swung the door open. I swallowed twice.

'Good morning, gentlemen.'

'Good morning.' I saw his glance go to the two vinyl Air France bags I was carrying together on one shoulder. He stepped aside and we went past him, down the stairway to our left.

The tempered glass doors of the safe-deposit room could not be seen all at once because the stairs took a ninety degree turn. My heart had begun to pound. When we reached the turn I could see the ersatz Dave Greeley standing with his back to us, checking his wristwatch. I swallowed again to moisten my dry mouth.

'Wait here till I get the door open,' I told Nico.

'Yeah.' He had placed the Beretta in his belt, just to one side of the buckle, and buttoned his jacket across it. If you weren't looking for a bulge, you wouldn't see it. Otherwise it was terribly apparent.

I left him hiding at the turn of the stairs and went to the glass door. When I rapped on it, the Greeley impersonator jumped. He turned and frowned at me. I decided this substitute was not much of a new business getter. I pointed to myself, smiled and pointed to my watch. His frown deepened but he unlocked the door.

'Remember me?' I began. 'You wouldn't let me in at three-thirty Friday?'

'Oh.' A pause. 'Yeah.' He swung the door open for me to come in. I did it slowly enough for Nico to come down the stairs and enter right behind me. The glass door swung briskly shut with the sharp click. Nine-thirty-one.

'You Dave Greeley?' I asked. Nico worked his way to one side of the bogus Greeley.

Before the man had a chance to lie, confess or even take a long breath, Nico's big right hand, open, chopped down sideways across the impersonator's neck. He dropped between us. I took his keys out of his hand. We hauled him quickly into the coupon-clipping room.

It's door had a lock that worked from the inside, so that customers could sequester themselves, but there was also a bolt on the outside. I checked to see if there was a telephone in the room, but found none. We bolted the door.

'Back up the stairs,' I told Nico. 'If anybody starts down, stall 'em. You dig?'

'Yeh.'

As we stood there, the vault time-release lock made a clicking noise and then emitted one short, discreet ping. With the door key, I let Nico out. Nine-thirty-two. I re-locked the door.

Then I marched myself back to the vault. This would be the only really tricky part. Along the way I found an empty safe-deposit box, one of those long, thin metal things. I swung open the vault door and there stood the most comical sight I'd seen since I arrived in London.

Harry Finch was small. He had probably been a jockey or, if not that, then a professional fake dwarf. He stood about four feet ten inches, most of it white with limestone dust. He stared at me with two round eyes and a mouth like an O. Nine-thirty-three.

'Harry Finch,' I told him, 'I'm Dave Greeley. Moe mentioned me.'

'Tell me why the fucking Embassy vault's still shut?'

'I don't know, Harry.'

'Fifty-four fucking hours in this fucking pesthole and no proper way out.' I looked down at his feet and saw the two loaded Air France flight bags.

'Are they the ones?' I asked.

'How the fuck would I know? I didn't open the fuckers.'

I stepped behind Harry and brought the safe-deposit box down as hard as I could on the back of his head. It only stunned him. He kept grumbling something as I picked him up under his arms and dragged him easily to the bolted door where Dave Greeley II slept. I shoved Harry in for company and re-bolted the door. It was risky, leaving them both that way. But what could they tell the police without incriminating themselves? Nine-thirty-four.

Then I ran back into the vault to the far end where Harry had neatly removed enough limestone for him to crawl through. I removed the wadded-up newspaper from my empty Air France bags and packed them with enough chunks of stone to give them some heft.

'Smash 'n' grab,' Jack Philemon announced from the Embassy side of the opening in the limestone. 'What makes you think Daddy can squeeze through this miniscule aperture?'

'Daddy doesn't have to,' I said, handing him Dorani's original flight bags. 'Off with you.'

'Who do you think you're bossing around?' he demanded. 'I'm ...' He consulted a folded piece of plasticized cardboard I'd given him over coffee early this morning. 'I'm Captain Paul Phelps, of US Army Intelligence, so I am.' He disappeared. I squinted through the opening in the wall and caught a glimpse of Clarissa Hudder — I imagine — securely trussed up in the vault on the other side. Jack seemed to have a foolproof way with the ladies. Nine-thirty-five.

I picked up my genuine sky blue Air France flight bags filled with costly limestone chunks and let myself out of the vault with the door key. Nico was standing just the other side of the ninety-degree turn in the stairs. 'What took y' so long?'

'Five minutes is long?'

We moved at a sprightly but not hurried pace up the stairs and past the bank guard. 'Good morning,' I said to him.

He touched his cap. 'Good morning to you, sir.' Nine-thirty-six.

We got in the cab at the same studied pace, not too fast, but slow enough so that I could see Jack Philemon leave the Embassy carrying a twenty-four-inch Samsonite travelling case with a combination lock. He wore a hat that hid most of his red hair. He hailed a cab that cut in ahead of us, delaying our departure a moment.

Then our driver steered us back to Blue's Hotel. We drove inside the little turnabout courtyard at precisely nine-fifty a.m.

'What's in the bags that's so important?' Nico muttered as we paid off the driver.

'Hot rocks.'

He gave me a dirty look, not realizing that for once I was levelling with him. I had felt rather easy once we'd locked the ersatz Dave Greeley away. No more dry mouth. No more difficulty extracting oxygen from the air. Once I'd seen the mini-sapper Moe had hired, I'd been fine.

Now my mouth had dried up again. I had the job of handing over two bags of nothing to a man who was counting on finding several million inside. I did have the sole clue to where his mistress was hiding but I couldn't expect that edge to last too long.

It never came to that.

It came to something a lot worse.

CHAPTER TWENTY-EIGHT

When we returned to Blue's, I had a certain reluctanc
to carry the rest of the farce through to its conclusion
'Okay,' I told Nico. 'My job's done. Take the bags up
stairs to Moe. I'll leave now and arrange for Rozzie t
come back here.'

Nico shook his head. 'My orders is not to let you outt
my sight. We both go upstairs.'

'It's the bags he wants, not me. Take them up.'

'No way,' Nico said, his face going mulish. 'Let's go.'

Which was why I was there during what happene
next. I suppose I could hardly have hoped, realistically
to avoid a scene of the sort. But I had no way of knowin
how it was destined to end.

Nico knocked at the door of Moe Gordon's suite. Afte
a moment a faint version of his voice called 'Come in.'

We did. The grandfatherly mobster sat lopsidedly o
his easy chair facing halfway between the door throug
which we came and the sofa on which Jean-Luc Dorar
sat.

I stopped short with so little warning that Nic
bumped into me. It didn't matter because our forwar
progress was totally halted when the broad-shouldere
man with long arms and thick neck appeared to one sid
of us, holding what seemed to be a .38 S&W magnur
with a silencer. This was a bit of a contradiction in itsel
because a magnum slug will tear the insides out of
silencer in two shots. But, then, all No-Neck needed wa
two shots.

He patted Nico down, removed the Beretta, whic

looked like a toy beside the magnum revolver, then frisked me and came up clean. He stepped back from us. Dorani indicated the bags with a graceful extension of his index finger.

'You needn't have gone to all the trouble, Mr Patrick,' he said in a faintly derisive voice. 'I would have been along in a while to withdraw them from the bank in the normal way. After all, they *are* mine.'

I glanced across at Moe Gordon. He sat silently, off centre, one leg crossed over the other, wrists crossed in his usual Jack Benny pose. He looked dead tired. There were lines around his huge eyes that hadn't been there before. But he was in control of himself, in a strangely hunched-over way.

'Jean-Luc,' he said, 'you don't think I had anything to do with this stunt.'

He pronounced it Gene-Luke, which wasn't too bad for an old hood who had stepped into something way over his head. His disclaimer didn't make much sense since, if I wasn't owned by him, Nico certainly bore the Gordon brand on his rump. I decided I had to play the cards I'd dealt myself. I marched the light blue flight bags forward and placed them on the floor beside Jean-Luc's neatly polished dark brown boots.

'Thank you,' he said, still in a mocking tone. 'I see you didn't take my advice.'

'I tried to,' I said, indicating Moe Gordon with a nod of my head. 'He wouldn't let me.'

Dorani threw back his head slightly and laughed, showing his teeth like a shark. 'Each of you disclaims the other. What difference does it make? I have these.' He nudged the flight bags with the toe of his boot.

'Fine,' I said. 'Can I go now?'

'I don't see how I can let you go,' he said with a certain derisive graveness, as if playing games with me. 'You and Mr Gordon have gone to a lot of trouble to steal my property. Even if I was intelligent enough to outguess you so that you brought the bags directly to

177

me, that doesn't wipe out what you tried to do.'

'Try not to think in terms of "we", can you?' I asked. 'A week ago I wasn't even *in* London, but this scam had already been set up. If you still have Greeley, you know what I'm saying is true.'

He pursed his lips and made a faint sound of tearing paper. My own lips were so dry they seemed to make a whispering noise when they rubbed against each other. I was having my usual trouble breathing. I tried to concentrate on living long enough with the symptoms of fear so that my body could rise above them.

'You were in New York, then,' Dorani granted me. 'Proving nothing. For all I know, he hired you to clean up whatever loose ends the Senate committee might come across in his absence.'

At the word 'Senate' I forgot I was having trouble with my breath. Another of my hunches had settled down on my shoulders. I had the sure feeling that I was going to get to the bottom of Moe Gordon and Rosalind Rue in the next few minutes. I might not, of course, last long enough for the knowledge to do anything much for me.

'Loose ends?' I said. 'The whole thing's unravelling. What do you think sent him into exile with the girl?'

Dorani grinned. 'I've seen her.'

'He's a dead man,' I said. 'Why does he need extra baggage on this trip? He's going home in a box.'

There was a long silence in the room. Then Moe Gordon sighed heavily. 'Yesterday a total stranger,' he told the air around him, 'today a *maven* on Moe Gordon.'

'On life expectancy,' I corrected him. 'Back in the States they want you dead. They don't want you doing your stand-up-guy routine before a Senate committee because they think you may spill more than you intended. You're unreliable. You're too full of secrets. You have to go.'

Dorani made a complicated that's-life gesture. 'You writers certainly have a way with words.'

'Don't you realize just how desperate he is?' I asked the Corsican. 'Moe Gordon, Mr Careful, tunnels into a bank vault to steal, of all things, *your* private war chest? Don't you recognize terminal insanity when you see it?'

'Terminal. Very good, that.'

'It's a getaway stake. He wants to drop off the face of the earth and that takes a lot of money.'

Dorani nudged the Air France bags with his toe again. 'You have no idea how much.' He brooded for a moment. 'What you say makes sense. An old man on the run, carrying with him the cause of his terror, carrying her with him into obscurity. It's a frightening vision.'

'Not as frightening,' I said, 'as if they'd subpoenaed *her*. Sooner or later they'd have to.'

'Oh?' He seemed only mildly interested.

'And despite the brainwashing he did on her, or she did on herself, she'd have to remember it finally and tell it, whatever it is they're trying to put together.'

Dorani's piercing eyes with their heavy slanted lids watched me for a long moment. Then his shark's smile grew sly and his voice mocking. 'But you don't really know what that is, do you, Mr Patrick?'

It was Moe Gordon who broke the silence then. 'Why should he know? There aren't five people alive today who know.'

'And after today?'

Gordon, frozen in his off-centre pose, looked at the Corsican. 'Jean, don't come on so heavy with an old friend. I did wrong to swipe your bundle. I admit it. You proved you were ten times smarter than me. I admit that, too. But you got your bundle back. Just let me clear out of your way and you'll never see me again. Fair enough?'

Dorani considered this for a moment with the same sly smile. 'No,' he said then. 'You have shown me a tremendous lack of respect. The news of it travels. So it must be followed by the news of what you paid for that disrespect.' He turned up the palms of his hands. 'You know as well as I there is no other way.'

Gordon, who had been sitting up somewhat jauntily, despite his fatigued sideways list, now settled slowly back into his chair. He closed his fawn's eyes and said no more.

'But you,' Dorani went on, turning to me, 'are another story. You are not one of us. You're a ... a freelance,' he managed to get a lot of contempt into the word. 'Before I decide what to do with you, tell me where you belong in this silly business.'

'I don't. I'm someone who was minding his own business and got involved with Rozzie. Met her at Fortune Films. She's supposed to have a part in a movie of my latest book. She visited me in my room. Then, later, I found her tied up, gagged and about to be shipped somewhere in a steamer trunk.'

Again Dorani threw back his head to laugh. 'Not only your books, but your anecdotes are most amusing.'

'Except the anecdote is not fiction. I got her out of the trunk and hid her away. That's where I fit into this silly business. Nowhere.'

Dorani turned to Gordon. 'What were you going to do with her?'

Gordon's eyes stayed shut. 'My affair.'

'But what he says is true?'

'Mostly.'

Dorani's hot glance swung back to me. 'And your plans for the lady? Are you perhaps carrying a subpoena with you? Do you want her back in Washington?'

'*I* don't,' I said.

'Pavel,' Dorani said to the man holding the magnum .38 S&W. A glance passed between them.

The broad-shouldered man pushed the muzzle of the silencer into Nico's back. 'Outside.' After they left we sat in silence for a moment. Much has been written about Mafia discipline, but whatever else it does it keeps patsies like Nico from raising a fuss on their way to a rub-out. In the tense silence, I wondered if I could —

I could. It sounded like the noise a whip makes passing by your ear, a kind of short vicious zzz. Exit Nico. I could hear a door open and close. Then the man with the .38 returned. 'To continue,' Dorani said then.

I indicated a chair. 'May I?'

'Certainly.'

I sat down opposite Moe Gordon, who rested perfectly still, eyes closed, as if in a coma. There was something about him that didn't look right. Perhaps being on the receiving end of tension and menace and the threat of death did that to a man. He looked warped out of perspective, as if sketched by an artist with astigmatism.

Then I saw what it was. Pavel, the no-neck man with the gun, hadn't frisked Moe Gordon. Gang chieftains like Moe don't carry guns. Top guys like Moe don't pull triggers. It shows lack of respect to pat them down. They're clean.

But Moe was, in fact, wearing Angie's Colt .45, tucked into his waistband over his hip. That was what was making him look as if he were strangely out of shape. That was why he hadn't really moved much. He was afraid to reveal the fact that, with any luck, he still hoped to blast his way out of this.

I had only two hopes: that he could still shoot straight and that he wanted Roz badly enough not to shoot me.

CHAPTER TWENTY-NINE

For a long while Dorani sat and watched all of us in turn with his basilisk eyes, as if memorizing the scene, but with the casual detachment of a theatregoer at a play he still doesn't care to understand too well.

The experienced Corsican had not seen what I'd noticed about Moe Gordon. I had prior knowledge that Foxy Grandpa had indeed soiled his hands with a gun long before Dorani had arrived. Now that the slap-happy Nico was no longer with us, perhaps I alone realized that after years of keeping clean, Moe Gordon had gone into the murder business again.

The idea of it was so bizarre that it wouldn't occur to Jean-Luc Dorani. He had concluded his calm survey of us by fastening his attention on me.

'So the woman has fallen in love with you.'

A flat statement didn't require an answer, but I knew I had to make a disclaimer if I didn't want to stop one of Moe Gordon's .45 slugs. 'She's still crazy about Moe. But she's upset at what he tried to do to her. I guess you could say their relationship is, um, going through a difficult period.'

Dorani nodded appreciatively. 'You have a droll way of putting things, Mr Patrick. But, then, I find your position in all of this exceeding droll. You have, by sheer bad luck or your misguided greed, blundered into an extremely serious situation, *comprenez-vous?* No one likes witnesses. Witnesses enjoy very short lives.'

'Leaving you to find Rosalind Rue without my help?'

He made one of his brushing-away gestures. 'You misread me, Mr Patrick. Gordon wants the woman. She is nothing to me.'

'Although in the States the families would pay to have her kept off the witness stand.'

'She has very little idea what she knows.'

'The Senate committee may think otherwise.'

'If they get what they want from Gordon, then what the girl can tell them becomes valuable. Not otherwise.'

He was telling me that I had no life insurance policy with him because I alone knew where Rozzie was. But I couldn't let it stand at that. I had to try changing his mind.

'Other friends of yours,' I said, 'besides the families. Powerful friends might like to talk to her. It would be an act of friendship and solidarity.' I paused for a moment only to try to take a breath and get rid of the waver I could hear in my voice. 'And in this European election year, it would be good insurance for your cause.'

Again he thought over what I'd said. 'You really don't know what you're talking about, do you, Mr Patrick?' His glance went to Moe Gordon for a moment. 'I think I shall tell you a story. A role reversal, isn't it? Usually I enjoy your narratives. But I don't think mine will bore you. Do you agree, Moe?'

'Dead men,' the old gangster said in his hoarse croak, 'don't tell no tales.'

'You see? He keeps his sense of humour. To the end.'

'They don't make them like Moe any more,' I said.

'You are a connoisseur of character,' the Corsican commented, 'and rather a devious character yourself, eh, Mr Patrick?'

'Not I.'

He nodded pleasantly, just as if no one had disagreed with me. 'For a novelist, you make a rather good thing out of crime.'

There was no answer to that. Anyway, as long as Pavel was holding the S&W magnum, his boss held the floor.

'In fact,' Dorani went on, 'on the basis of revenue

alone, you have a way of making one crime pay twice, *n'est ce pas?* You plan it. You commit it. Then you change around the details and you write it as fiction.' He chuckled. It was a chilling sound. 'And you have been doing this for some time now. Am I right?'

'Are you ever wrong?' I asked in what I hoped was a soothing voice.

'But why? Is it only for the money?'

'It's a form of therapy. I had a rough time after I left Uncle's employ. Bad dreams. I thought they came from the memory of the things I had done for Uncle. But that was a mistake.' I stopped talking, not wanting to take his podium from him.

'Go on, please.'

'The reason I was having trouble was that I had designed a new identity for myself at odds with what I really was.'

Dorani gave me a shark-like smile of such complicity that I wondered for a moment what I was doing explaining myself to this scavenger. But, then, who was I to make value judgements?

'I realized that I was a thief,' I said then.

Nobody said anything for a while. Dorani's smile grew, if anything, even more intimidatingly pally. 'A thief,' he echoed then.

'No way of knowing if I'd started that way, or if Uncle had turned me into one,' I continued. 'The main thing was to recognize what I was, stop fighting it and start cashing in.'

'A thief.' His smile faded. 'You know the fate of the thief who is on his own? The unaffiliated thief?'

I nodded. 'But Shakespeare,' I said then, 'says it's important to be true to thine own self.'

He sat there and examined me minutely for a while, at his leisure, the purveyor of what was going to pass for justice in this room. 'Such an accomplished story-teller,' he mused aloud. 'Such a mistake, putting it aside for simple thievery.' He glanced at Moe Gordon. It was an almost physical relief not to be under his scrutiny, even if only for a moment.

'My old friend, Moe,' the Corsican said solemnly. 'Shall I tell your story to this story-teller? Perhaps he will steal it for one of his novels.'

Gordon produced a sound halfway between a laugh and a grunt of pain. 'Somehow I don't figure he'll get the chance.'

Dorani moved about to a more comfortable position on the sofa. In so doing, he touched the blue flight bags again with the toe of his boot. 'It was one of the Caribbean islands, Cuba, that Mr Gordon and his associates used during Prohibition as an entrepôt for liquor. They had established its capital, Havana, as Sin City of the Western Hemisphere. Whatever one wanted in the world of sex was for rent in Havana.

'After the Second World War, their investment became even more substantial. Drugs, gambling, guns. But also real estate and industry. They invested millions to reap profits of billions. This little island ninety miles off Florida was the moneymaking Hope diamond in their tiara.'

He paused to consider his own flair for imagery. His taut, dark face with its hungry eyes and high forehead had grown mysteriously animated as he talked. I had the feeling he was trying to impress me with his story-telling powers. He was having one hell of a success.

'And then, the unthinkable. Castro came down from the hills and swept everyone, including Mr Gordon, away. He literally had forty-eight hours to get out of Havana. One doesn't lightly abandon a source of billions in profit. He and his associates began planning immediately for the recovery of their investment. Since 1940, they had helped to elevate a young attorney until he was now vice president under a totally easy-going president.'

He glanced at the man whose past history he had been summarizing. The little old grandpa sat with his eyes closed. I noticed he had tucked his hand inside his jacket,

Napoleon style, as if his abdomen was giving him trouble. I wondered if, in fact, he actually had the Colt .45 automatic in his grip.

'I think you know what happened after that,' Dorani went on. 'A considerable force, mostly Mr Gordon's former employees, had been gathered on a coffee plantation in Guatemala. Your CIA had provided guns and a political cover story that these were Cuban patriots. The vice president was now running for the presidency and his first act would, of course, be to unleash this invasion force on Cuba. But when he lost to Mr Kennedy, he sought and received several private audiences with him, trying to persuade him to expedite the Cuban invasion. Its success was based on three factors, two of them illusions. The first illusion was that the invasion force was a well-trained commando group when in fact it was riddled with mutinous malcontents. The second was that the Cuban people would rise against Castro when the invasion force struck. A false dream. But the third factor of success was a least a possibility. Your CIA had B-26 attack bombers in Nicaragua. These planes would provide air cover.'

He glanced down at the Air France flight bags. Something had caught his attention. He reached over and flicked away a whitish speck, having no idea it was limestone dust.

'Kennedy was on the spot and badly advised,' Jean-Luc went on. 'He was damned if he did and damned if he didn't. So he gave the invasion a green light. After all, he could justify the men. They were largely Cubans and one could twist their mission into a patriotic one. But there was no way to explain the B-26s and so, at the last instant, Kennedy called off the air cover. The rest you know. The invaders died on the beaches. The plan for retaking Cuba died with them.'

He turned towards Moe Gordon. 'If you were Mr Gordon, or one of his mainland associates, you would be very angry with President Kennedy. But you would live with your anger. What cannot be cured must be endured, *n'est ce pas?* On the other hand, suppose you had reason to believe you had an agreement with the president? A deal for air cover. In that case, what he did would not be merely inconvenient. It would have been an act of treachery.'

The word echoed strangely in the airless hotel suite. Moe Gordon's eyes opened slowly and he stared at Dorani almost without seeing him, as if gazing into the past.

'There is only one penalty for treachery,' the Corsican said at last. 'It was delivered as soon as it could be arranged, two years later ... in Dallas.'

He and Moe Gordon watched each other with tired wariness, as if neither were a novelty to the other, but only a tricky reality that had to be outguessed. 'Have you suspected the rest?' Dorani asked. 'Is it clear how the air cover deal was consummated? The intermediary who carried the terms back and forth between Gordon and Kennedy? Without understanding what she was doing, I am sure.'

'Incredible.'

'*D'accord,*' he agreed.

'But this man set her up for it,' I said then, looking at Moe Gordon. 'This man took a sixteen-year-old kid and groomed her for precisely this job. He taught her everything she needed to know and then put her next to Kennedy a dozen ways until she clicked. Until she was running back and forth between beds, carrying pillow talk from the President of the United States to the Chairman of the Board of the Syndicate.'

The elderly mobster produced a small, almost shy smile. 'If I tell you I had nothing to do with bringing them together. If I say it was an accident and I was jealous as hell about it. If I tell you —'

'We wouldn't believe it,' Dorani cut in. 'You cast about among your little actresses and singers and put a few of them beside Kennedy until one struck his fancy. As simple as that.'

I sat without speaking for a while, digesting the whole idea. As hard as it was to swallow, I knew it answered a lot of questions. 'And now it's all going to spill out,' I said then.

Gordon shrugged. 'Not without me to confirm it. Without me the Senate can't prove nothing. You know what? They're just as happy. Nobody wants to unleash that kind of *dreck* on the public.'

'Could be,' I agreed. 'The government isn't any more eager to uncover the Cuban connection than you are. Which is why —' I stopped myself. Which is why, I repeated silently, you have to be hit, Moey. Why this whole set-up was arranged in the beginning. To lure you in and wipe you out.

Gordon's eyes got a shiny, self-righteous look. 'The public can only take so much. After all, sonny, you're overlooking the national security side of this. And don't leave out what the CIA did to move it along. Taking Cuba away from Castro would have saved us the whole missile crisis.'

'A patriot.' I heard the word I had spoken rattle into the corners of the suite. 'Moe Gordon, patriot to the end. Throwing away his own selfish interests. Fleeing the US for the good of his adopted motherland.'

'You could say that,' the tired old man said.

I turned to Dorani. 'Do you believe it?'

'A persuasive argument. I myself have taken similar positions at times. What do they say about patriotism?' He smiled a shade too broadly and his jaw showed white, pointed teeth.

'I can tell the whole story a different way,' I said then. 'I can tell it so it accounts for his desperate moves. A desperation that made him try to steal your property. His associates, like himself, have become so respectable, so firmly entrenched in the establishment, so *legal*, that they have to destroy this living memento of their own past misdeed. Especially the Kennedy hit. Moe's an anachronism, an embarrassing one. Dinosaurs have to die.'

No one spoke. My own words echoed in my ears. They got mixed up with something Moe had said about the CIA's complicity in the Bay of Pigs. I glanced at Dorani's hooded, thoughtful face.

If I wanted to stay alive, I had to keep Dorani thinking that I blamed the families for Moe's present plight. If he suspected I knew that Uncle had given him the original contract on Moe Gordon, my life was forfeit.

As it was, I didn't really give any great odds on my staying alive. By bungling into Dorani's deal with Uncle, I had turned it from a simple hit to a complicated set of criss-cross betrayals. The fact that Dorani had felt free to speak of the Cuban matter before me was as chilling an indication as I needed that he already considered me a dead man.

Something in my face seemed to stir him to speak again. He sat forward suddenly in his chair.

'I have a fraternal duty,' he said, 'to my associates in America. I don't see it extending to the woman. Her protector,' he eyed Gordon, 'is another matter.' His glance shifted to the stocky man with the .38 magnum. 'Pavel?'

Gordon made his move. The action was smooth enough, for elderly muscles and reflexes, but the noise was appalling. The Colt .45 kicked once in his right hand. Pavel toppled forward, a small stain on his lower abdomen and his rear end splattered against the wall. The smell was nauseating.

Gordon was on his feet, scrambling for Pavel's silenced .38. He came up with it and levelled it at Dorani. He had scorched a hole in his expensive jacket, but otherwise he looked hale and hearty. 'Let's hope nobody paid no attention to that blast.'

His big doe's eyes looked pained, perhaps at the thought of what he had to do next.

CHAPTER THIRTY

I shall never forget the look in Jean-Luc Dorani's eyes, those hooded eyes that had witnessed so much of the world's treachery and violence.

And yet he seemed profoundly shocked. It hadn't occurred to him, nor had he been forewarned, that one of his own high level of master managers would stoop so low as to carry a gun and use it.

Make no mistake about it. Dorani had killed. There was no way a young, ambitious Corsican could have risen to power except by exterminating the people in his way. But that was the past, buried beneath decades of outward respectability, wreathed in garlands of alibis and deceptions meant to protect him forever from culpability.

For even longer, Moe Gordon had enjoyed that same bland insulation from the messy events that lie at the heart of the smoothest business transactions, the bullet in the stomach, the wire at the throat. Or much more powerful, the *threat* of death.

Perhaps only now, as he stared down at the shattered, reeking body of his broad-shouldered bodyguard, did Dorani understand how dangerous a man Moe Gordon had become. 'Fool,' he muttered then, but whether it was meant for Gordon or himself no one knew. 'Damned fool.'

Then I understood. He was only addressing the dead man. He was only being practical, not philosophical. Pavel hadn't frisked the old man because he'd relied on the time-honoured code. He'd been wrong to trust any-one, even a man as high up as Moe Gordon. Perhaps *especially* such a man. So Pavel had died ... for his trustingness.

With a finicky movement of his foot, Dorani pushed the flight bags in Gordon's direction.

'Now it's armed robbery,' he said in his earlier, mocking tone. 'And it's I who have been outguessed by you.'

Moe's big soft eyes fixed for an instant on the Air France bags. 'One thing left to do,' he said then. 'Sonny, I want my little girlie. I give you half an hour to get her here.'

I got to my feet. 'What makes you think I won't keep on walking?'

Moe Gordon extended the toe of his small, neat loafer until it touched the flight bag nearest him. 'We still got a deal. Bring me the girlie and you take away one of the bags.' His glance shifted upwards to my face. 'I know you, sonny. You'll be back.'

I nodded gravely, turned to Dorani and nodded again. '*A bientôt*,' I said.

'I shall be dead when you return,' the Corsican told me matter-of-factly.

'Surely not.'

'As surely as he would have been.' His shark's smile flashed for an instant. The stench from Pavel's body was appalling.

I watched him for a long moment, trying to find in his face a sign of what he was, of the terrifyingly simple murder he'd been paid so much to arrange, and by an employee of such awesome prestige. The price had been great, but the need to silence Moe Gordon had been greater. I'd been a fool to think his death had meant so much to the mob. It had meant much, much more to Uncle.

I stepped over Pavel on my way to the door. 'Half an hour,' I told Moe Gordon.

Downstairs in the lobby I got them to open my safe-deposit box. Then I left the hotel. Outside the April morning was clear, the air clean. I took a breath of it.

I walked to a telephone booth, called the police and reported murders on the fourth floor of Blue's. I mentioned only two.

CHAPTER THIRTY-ONE

On my way to Heathrow Airport I tried to trace any loose ends and probe soft spots. Having called in the police, what could I expect them to turn up?

Bodies, of course. Nico's and Pavel's at least. Probably Dorani's by the time they got to the hotel. Moe Gordon would be left together with several guns that had his fingerprints on them, and two Air France flight bags filled with top quality limestone chunks.

By now, too, the police would have been called in at the Manhattan Bank and Trust Company, Mayfair Branch. A customer would have tried to get to his safe-deposit box and found no one in attendance. The bank officers would eventually have discovered two men locked in the customer's room. One man had no business there, little Harry Finch. It probably wouldn't take the police more than a day to establish that the man calling himself Dave Greeley wasn't.

The tunnelling job would be discovered by now. Very possibly they would be able to crack Clarissa and get her to implicate ... Moe Gordon. Her story about the mysterious Captain Paul Phelps would lead the police nowhere. Jack had kept his hat on, so there wasn't even the clue of his red hair to follow. Nor would the Samsonite case prove useful since it was far too common a piece of luggage.

Eventually, I felt sure, the bogus Dave Greeley and Harry Finch, the sapper, would produce descriptions of me, which would tally, I suppose, with the bank guard's recollection of how I looked. But I'm not that easy to describe, as I've said before. I look like a lot of people. It's damned useful.

What did that leave, I wondered as the cab raced out along the motorway to the airport? Moe Gordon alive in his hotel room with bags of rocks that tracked back to the hole tunnelled through the wall. No real fingerprints at the scene from either Jack or me. Which left it all with Moe. Would he bring me into his story? It was certainly possible.

Angie, too, was a loose end. But if his name didn't appear in the police investigation of the Blue's Hotel murders, why would he surface, despite his itch to implicate me? He'd have to expose himself in so doing and even Angie wasn't that stupid.

That left Rosalind Rue. She had been my good luck charm throughout all this. Knowing where she was had given me an edge with her elderly protector. Perhaps it would still keep him from weaving my name into whatever story he told.

Finally, there was the one unknowable factor ... Uncle.

As soon as Blue-Eyes learned that Moe Gordon was alive and Dorani's vault had been looted – and he might in fact already have heard about it from the Embassy side of the caper – he'd take it hard. But without Dorani to tie me into it, Blue-Eyes had no reason to want my head. Of course, if Dorani by some miracle got away alive—

We had reached the place where roads branch out to various parts of the airport. 'Which terminal, sir?' the driver asked.

'International departures.'

At the terminal building. I made my way to the waiting area upstairs. Jack Philemon, his red hair visible across the room, was reading a magazine filled with photos of breasts and vulvas. He didn't glance away from it as I sat down beside him.

'Took your bloody time, didn't you?' he muttered.

'Sorry.'

'The Samsonite bag,' he said, 'went on Air France Flight 801. It'll be in De Gaulle Airport about now. When you don't claim it, they'll shuffle it over to Held luggage. You'll have a week to reclaim it. Please do. Otherwise they force it open and, as you Yanks so gracefully put it, the shit hits the fan.'

I took the magazine from him and glanced at the centrefold colour photo of a girl in a red flannel hat teasing herself with a red-striped peppermint candy cane. I covered her with two packets of hundred-dollar bills from my hotel lock box. Then I closed the magazine and handed it back to Jack.

'That magazine's old stuff. Must be the Christmas issue.'

He put it under his arm as he got to his feet. 'Here's your claim check for the bag,' he said, handing over an unused London–Paris ticket with the little baggage coupon stapled to it.

I stood up next to him. 'Jack, as always a pleasure working with you.'

He nodded. 'How many dunderheads could you find in this town who'd take a fistful of hundred dollar bills instead of Sweet Christ knows how many thousand-franc Swiss notes.'

'Oh, you looked in the flight bags?'

'Nothing of the sort. Daddy's nosy, but Daddy's discreet.'

'Just guessed?'

He nodded. 'It's called extrapolation in my circle.' He started to say something more, but saw that my attention had swung elsewhere.

It had, in fact, swivelled to a bright red woman's cape, a regular Little Red Ridinghood cloak, which was making its way towards the International Departure lounge. It was Jane Tait's cape, but the legs beneath it were not Jane's, nor was the tousled head of sable hair that showed above it.

In fact, the woman in Jane Tait's cape was about six inches too short for it. 'Has Daddy got any friends at Heathrow?' I asked Jack.

'Daddy is universally beloved.' His glance had swung to follow mine. 'Fancy that, do you?'

It took him a telephone call. Then Jack escorted me on a circuitous route I'd never be able to remember again, up elevators and down ramps until we were in the big departure lounge to one side of the free shops, staring through a wall of plate glass at Rosalind Rue, who was buying a flacon of 'Vivara'.

She tucked it into the oversized leather bag Jane Tait usually carried for manuscripts. Then she sat down near the big announcement board, pulled her collar up around her, readjusted her dark glasses and tried to look inconspicuous. She almost succeeded.

'Keep an eye on her while I make a call?' I asked Jack.

'No charge.' He grinned at me. 'Do you get the same feeling I do? That under the coat she's got nothing on?'

'Hold the thought.'

I telephoned Jane Tait's office, only to be told she was working at home today.

I dialled her home number. There wasn't even one double bz-bz. At a single bz the telephone was snatched off its hook. 'Yes?' Jane Tait demanded.

'It's me. I'm sorry I couldn't call before.'

'Dear God,' she breathed. 'I have been going looney for the last hour.'

'What happened?'

'Everything,' she reported in an end-of-rope voice. 'I went out to get some buns for our breakfast. I was gone fifteen minutes, Max. And she bolted.'

'How? In what?'

'Took my cape, my passport, a tenner from my wallet *and* my American Express card.'

'No note?'

'But of course. Let us never assume that this sawed-off nymphomaniacal bitch doesn't have manners.'

I let a moment of silence slip by. 'Emma Jane Tait,' I said then in a reproving tone.

'Let me read her note. "Dearest J., off to south of France. Will airmail all your things back to you soonest. Thanks for everything. Take care of Max. Love, Roz." Is that cheek? Is that gall?'

'You'll get everything back. She's, um, money-honest.'

' "Take care of Max." It chills the blood, that kind of nerve.'

'Will you?'

'What?' she demanded. 'Take care of Max? I need care, not you.'

'Can you take the week off, Emma Jane?'

There was a longish pause. 'To what avail?'

'Trip to Paris. The Alsace, if you like. I also need a day in Zurich. Otherwise, write your own itinerary.'

'Anywhere but the French Riviera.'

'Promise.'

'What shall I tell Ian at the office?'

'Feeling seedy. Need a holiday.'

'He'd never agree,' she said. 'What if you've just given me a new manuscript and I want to lock up for a week and go over it?'

'Emma Jane, you're getting to be an accomplished liar.'

'It's just the nearness of you,' she murmured and hung up.

When I got back to the lounge, Jack had moved up near one of the checkpoints through which departing passengers go when their flight is called. On the overhead announcement board a red light was blinking next to BA 076 for Nice. Roz had gathered Jane Tait's bag and was on her feet.

I signalled over the heads of the crowd that I didn't want Jack to stop her. He was standing perhaps two feet from her as she showed her boarding pass and walked through in search of the departure gate for her flight. I got to the checkpoint in time to see her disappear around a corner of a walkway, a fine figure of a woman, even in the wrong cape.

'Be still, my heart,' Jack murmured.

Someone nearby chuckled. I turned and found Curly smiling at me. He'd remembered the red sweater now but, instead of folding it around his waist, he had it draped over his back with the arms knotted under his chin. Joe Tennis.

I was near enough to Curly, and to Jack, so that I could take each one by the arm and move them out of the crush around the checkpoint.

'Cuppa coffee?'

Neither man seemed terribly surprised that we were now a threesome. I led the way to the fast-food cafeteria section. I suppose we looked peculiar to anyone watching us. None of us spoke as we filed through. Each of us took it a different way: me, black, Curly with cream and sugar, Jack choosing a pot of tea. Still not speaking, we agreed without words on a table that was surrounded by a cordon of empty tables.

Predictably, it was Curly who broke the silence. 'What's Miss Tait going to do in Nice?' was the way he put it. 'Vacation?'

Jack Philemon, who knew Jane Tait from having been at one of her parties, gravely sipped his tea. 'Sort of,' I agreed then. 'Why were you following her?'

'The cape, man. I had you that first day at Shepherd Market, you know. She was wearing the cape. And, yesterday, I picked you up coming from her apartment. Simple.'

I stared at him. Surely he had to know that the woman in the bright red cape was not the woman he'd seen wearing it at Shepherd Market. But there was no way I could ask him about it without contributing to his education. He didn't wait to be asked.

'That wild black thing's a wig,' he said with a sure air of confidence. 'Man, nobody's got real hair like that.'

I nodded contemplatively, thinking that an air of confidence is everything these days. Probably Jane Tait had been sitting down when he'd first seen her at Shepherd Market, so he had no idea how tall she was. But how had he missed seeing Rosalind Rue that same day, since she was on the arm of Moe Gordon?

I decided Uncle had assigned Curly to me and no other. If Ghengis Khan had come between us riding his foam-flecked pinto at the head of a horde of ravening Mongols lusting to destroy Western Civilization, a time-serving servant like Curly would still follow Max Patrick and his editor-girlfriend-whatever. Wherever. And whoever.

'Can I ask you something?' I began then. 'Why are you still on me? Didn't I satisfy Blue-Eyes yesterday?'

His smile got positively chummy. 'Blue-Eyes! That's a gas! He's on his way back to Langley right now, heading for the hot seat.'

I digested this slowly, wondering how much of it Jack understood. Langley, Virginia, is home base for a lot of Uncle's farflung Intelligence webs. I wondered how long Curly's fit of talkativeness would last.

'Why's he on the griddle?' I asked. Then I got a sudden inspiration. 'Don't tell me you guys are bankrolling Dorani.'

Curly cackled silently. I don't know if this manoeuvre is easy for you to picture. It's an old vaudeville routine that lads Curly's age must have picked up from kids' television shows. One silently pantomimes 'yuck-yuck-yuck'. It's meant as sarcasm, I think.

'And it was Blue-Eyes' idea,' I supplied then. 'No wonder he's sweating blood. His head's on the block, huh?'

Curly's eyes went up into his head in an oh-wow-is-it! gesture. 'But why are you still messing around with me?' I asked.

Curly's hands went to his sides, shoulders high, palms

up. 'I don't have a rescind on you, yet. Maybe tomorrow.'

'Then somebody else is watching Dorani?'

'Man, what kind of budget do you think we have on this?' The young man sounded almost huffy, as if husbanding the American taxpayer's dollar was his responsibility alone.

I sighed, more with relief than chagrin. It was impossible to be angry with such stupidity. There was a budget from which immense sums could be filtered through Dorani to Europe's right-wing parties. And, with a certain prim Calvinist logic, the funds could also serve as bloodmoney for the death of Moe Gordon. But there wasn't enough budget to assign two field agents to protect the money. Just poor, overworked, time-serving Curly.

'Can we give you a lift back to town?' I asked, getting to my feet.

Curly choked down some of his super-sweetened coffee and managed to shake his head negatively at the same time. Jack stood up with me. 'You drove that damned Mini here, didn't you?' I asked the lad.

He glanced up at me with something like good-natured guilt. 'Hey, man, I'm sorry about the other day. It was accidental.'

'That I survived, you mean.'

'Listen, I didn't even know you'd be crossing there. I lost you at Piccadilly and I was just zooming around those damned one-way streets hoping to pick you up again. I rounded the corner and ... whammo!'

I managed to take all this in without betraying any of the things I was feeling. Relief was still uppermost. If Curly had no order to hit me, then I was in a much better position vis-à-vis Uncle. With Blue-Eyes back in the States and in trouble, my position had improved even more.

'See you,' I said, turning to leave.

Of all the things he might have said to me – or remained mute – Curly then chose the one phrase that might some day get me to renounce US citizenship, the phrase every shopgirl gives you with the receipt for your purchase.

'Have a nice day,' he said, grinning up at me. And meant it.

CHAPTER THIRTY-TWO

If I'd followed my normal instincts, I would have said good-bye to Jack at Heathrow and let him get back to town under his own power. But I was feeling a little fragile, a little like destiny's plaything. After all, in my unwritten agreement with Uncle there was no clause that said only good-natured idiots would always be assigned to me.

In an hour or two I would have rounded up Jane Tait and we'd be leaving London, probably by car or train, any mode of transport but too-closely-checked aircraft traffic. It was good-bye to London for some time.

Jack and I walked downstairs by a circuitous route that somehow bypassed customs and immigration, emerging on the street level where cabs unloaded passengers.

We stood there, awkwardly. I considered Jack a friend, but we'd never behaved with each other as much more than client and hired hand. His glance went past me to a dark-brown taxi waiting at the back of the unloading cabs. 'Hullo. Maybe he's free.'

We walked over to the cab. 'Teddy,' Jack said. 'Got a fare?'

The driver sat for a moment in silence. Then he shrugged. 'You'll do, Jack.' We got in and gave him no directions except to return to town. We sat back and stretched our legs. Jack ran his finger through his springy red hair. He was showing the night's lack of sleep, his skin more blotched with green colour than usual. I supposed I didn't look that stunning, either.

'Who was that clot in the café? Some bizarre protégé of yours?'

'By no means.'

'Then you're not still ...' He paused for a discreet way of asking the question. However, there is no discreet way.

'I'm not working for Uncle, haven't for almost six years.'

'Then why did Smiley-Face open up that way?'

'Because that's the nature of Smiley-Faces all over the world.'

Jack shook his head. 'I don't understand it, I don't. Isn't there some sort of screening process that keeps Uncle, as you call him, from hiring dimwits?'

'Oh, it's gone far beyond that,' I assured him. 'That lad has been trained by dimwits. He's second generation dimwit. Probably can't spell, either.'

Jack's laugh sounded rueful and malicious at the same time. I suppose nothing warms the cockles of a Brit's secret heart more than seeing a big, overbearing friend like the United States revealed as a collection of self-perpetuating incompetents.

'But that's only because he's come up the college way,' I warned Jack. 'Uncle has a whole other team recruited from the streets. What they lack in schooling they supply in smarts.'

'From what streets?'

'Stoolies, undercover men, hoods who've turned into informers. They make excellent agents, most of them.'

'*Quis custodiat, ipsos custodies?*'

The nice thing about Jack, apart from his total efficiency, is that he never tries to remind one that he did in fact take a history honours at Oxford. Only in moments of stress does any of it show. As now.

'Knock it off,' I demurred. 'We gave up watching the watchers years ago.' This remark had the effect of plunging both of us into gloom for the next quarter of an hour while the taxi negotiated the motorway back to London through gradually thickening traffic.

'You can let me off at Blue's Hotel,' I leaned forward to tell the driver.

When he spoke it was out of the corner of his mouth, addressing the small opening in the glass barrier. 'Just come from S'n Jymes's,' he volunteered. 'Proper dustup. Police vans all over the plyce.'

Jack seemed to shift out of his fit of depression. 'What's the story, Ted?'

'Two stories. Bank robbery over in Mayfair. And four dead 'uns at Blue's, so the starter told me. The whole place is one great traffic jam.'

Four!

I ignored Jack's sidelong look at me. Pavel and Nico would be two of the corpses and Dorani was surely the third. But then ...

I could picture Moe Gordon waiting in the silence of his suite, surrounded by bodies. Waiting for me to appear with Rozzie. The tension would be high. Just to help time pass, he would open the flight bags to count the money.

One look at those chunks of limestone and he would know he had no place to go. He'd remember his own advice: 'dead men don't tell no tales'. The muzzle of the Colt would taste foul as he put it in his mouth. But that would only last a second or two.

'Maybe we'd better stay out of the area,' I heard myself telling the driver. 'Just take me to West Ken.' I turned to Jack. 'Where can I drop you?'

There was something cold in his glance before he looked away. 'Daddy wants out right here,' he muttered. We were passing through a wasteland of small factories and warehouses. 'I had no idea you were into anything as heavy as four stiffs.'

'I don't even carry a piece,' I said in an undertone. 'Goddamn it, Jack, you know me better than that.'

His glance swung back to me, slowly, almost unwillingly. 'Do I?'

I let it go. Jane Tait was probably right about me. I did keep people at arm's length, as I had Jack. And it was just as well, wasn't it? What did one get if one narrowed the gap? Regrets? I'd just paid the man quite well for some minor offences – breaking and entering, impersonating an officer, exporting stolen funds. I'd made the mistake of thinking that a good fee also bought him as a comrade-in-arms. But not with four dead ones on hand.

'All right, Jack. You can stop the cab anywhere along here.'

For a long moment he said nothing. Then: 'Feeling much put-upon?' When I glanced at him he was grinning evilly.

'Just a bit disappointed.'

'Substandard services?'

'Today's service was perfect. It's today's attitude.'

He shook his head and glanced warningly at the driver. 'I'm only worth your money,' he said in a very low voice, 'if I still have the run of this town.' His big eyes watched me closely.

It really was a classic situation. I'd chosen a life in which there couldn't be friends, not real ones, only business associates. Of course there was Jane Tait, who'd begun as a business associate and was now— What?

We were moving slowly through thickening London traffic, even this far from the busy centres of the city. Jack cleared his throat and started to say something, then stopped. He laughed softly, under his breath, and tried again.

'This Uncle of yours,' he said then.

'Not mine.'

'Well, you and all the other feckless sods who pay US taxes.' He stopped again and glanced at me to see if I were still holding him at arm's length. He decided, I guess, that I wasn't. 'I gather,' he went on, 'that Uncle was using the Corsican connection as a conduit for European political payoffs?'

'Something like that,' I admitted, not wanting to add the Gordon hit to it.

'They've been using the Mafia that way for eons.' He was silent a moment. 'Is that the lolly I shipped to Paris for you?'

'Something like that.'

'Communication with you is a one-way street,' he responded in a dry voice. 'In any event, old fellow, I'm sure it's crossed your mind that Dorani isn't the only pipeline Uncle has for feeding plasma into the right-wing parties of Europe. Just one artery among many, I judge.'

'Something —' I stopped myself. Even I could see how ugly I had started behaving. 'The part that hurts,' I got out then, 'is that Uncle uses people for other things, too. It's no longer possible to tell the difference between a low grade button-man like Curly, the one you had tea with just now, and, let's say, one of the Corsican brand.'

'Except that Curly just talks and talks.' Jack's voice got dreamy. 'He'd be a love under interrogation, eh?' Then, in the same artless tone: 'How much did you lift? A million or so?'

It was almost a physical struggle to keep from saying 'Something like that.' Instead I swallowed and said: 'Yes.'

'Not to worry, chum. Not to fret one's tiny head.' He gave me a friendly punch in the forearm. 'Look at it this way: the swag you lifted is about one twentieth the cost of a single F-14 fighter plane.'

I stared at him glumly. His arithmetic was flawless. While the whole pack of us had schemed and manoeuvred and taken chances and broken laws and sweated a bit of blood – and died – Uncle was calmly trading away twenty times as much with every obsolete fighter plane he flogged to some oil-rich sheikh.

'Which gives you an idea,' Jack went on with surgical

calm, 'how much more of Uncle's loose change is still around for people like Dorani to funnel into European elections.'

'Christ.'

'I'm proud to know you, son,' he said. 'Just rubbing up against you makes Daddy feel rich and tinkly inside.'

'Any time.'

He looked at me for a moment and all the bantering went out of his face, as if, for an instant, he'd dropped his own arm-length's defences. 'Ah, well,' he said then, with a dying fall.

We got out in West Kensington and I paid off the driver. 'Thanks for not taking me into S'n Jymes's, guv,' he said. I added a pound-note tip. 'Much obliged. 'F you ask me, them murders was a crime of passion.'

I stared at him and I'm afraid my mouth was open. He saluted us and drove off. I watched the cab disappear in heavy traffic along Kensington High Street. Crime of passion?

Thinking of the woman on Flight 076 for Nice, I decided the driver was right.

I turned to Jack to say good-bye.

But he was gone.

Economic analysis, *Neue Zurcher Zeitung*, 9 March:

Decades ago the American novelist Sinclair Lewis envisioned a fascist coup in a book called *It Can't Happen Here*. For as many decades, European business leaders have viewed the takeover of the American economy by criminals with the smug self-assurance, 'it can't happen here'. But the alliance between European and American crime syndicates was also forged decades ago, with the heroin traffic routes as its pattern. Today these routes operate in reverse. Money and political power move eastward to Europe at an ever-mounting rate. It is happening ... here.